THE COFFIELD CHRONICLES
HEARTS UNDER SIEGE - BOOK ONE

THE COFFIELD CHRONICLES
HEARTS UNDER SIEGE - BOOK ONE

TL DICKERSON

SAPPHIRE BOOKS

SALINAS, CALIFORNIA

Dedication

I dedicate this novel to Angie Ramirez, my sweet mother. My mom wanted very much for me to write this story. It was her idea to blend my two loves of history and romance. She was an avid Historical Romance reader, sometimes reading up to five books a week. It took me a year and a half to write The Coffield Chronicles (Hearts Under Siege and its sequel Hearts Under Fire), and during the final pages of creation, my mother found out that she had a rather large aneurism in her aorta. Time became of the essence and I was able to finish writing it. I couldn't even give her a polished draft to read. It was raw and unedited but she read it to the end, completing it just a week before she passed away. She loved it and told me her thoughts on it. I don't think I could have lived with myself had she not been able to finish reading it. But the universe has a way of making sure things happen as they're supposed to, and for that I'm thankful. Thank you, Mom, for being my best friend and always supporting me in my writing. Mostly, thank you for loving me. This one's for you!

Acknowledgment

I'd like to start by thanking my wife, Gail Breslin, for giving me that push I needed to get back into writing in the first place. Her support and encouragement have been a bedrock for my writing, allowing me that safe place to shed my heart into words. She's the best wife ever.

A huge shout out and thank you to Heather Flournoy for not only being such a great editor but for taking me under her wing. I've learned a lot already just from the short amount of time we've worked together. You have a way of explaining things in such a way that it's almost impossible to misunderstand. That put me at such ease that I had no problem delivering what you asked for, and I appreciate it more than you know.

A heartfelt thank you to Chris Svendsen, publisher of Sapphire Books, for taking a chance on me and this story. It's been my life's dream to be a published author. I needed to know if my writing was good enough for someone to publish, and that question has now been answered. I appreciate the opportunity.

I'd also like to thank Colleen Decicco and Debi Wagner for helping propel me to this point of getting published by Sapphire Books. The time you both took out of your busy lives to help ensure the best draft of the story I could send out to Sapphire is much appreciated and must be noted. Thank you.

Lastly, I'd like to thank my father, Henry Ramirez, for his immeasurable support of my sought-after writing career. You set the groundwork for me, setting that example of going after your dreams and staying focused by not listening to the naysayers of the world. I love you, Dad.

Chapter One

Dark, looming clouds tore across the late afternoon sky, threatening to impede our normal routine of herding in the cattle. Rounding them back up and leading them back into the barn was a dreaded chore. At age fifteen, and being the scrawny tomboy that I was, fighting the wind while riding my horse and corralling cattle through a now pelting rain was no easy task. But proving my capability and strength to my father was always foremost in my mind.

"Melody, go around," he said, doing his best to help me guide the filthy, wet beasts through the barn doors.

Angus Coffield was not only my father, he was a good man who worked hard, and I respected his integrity. He was my favorite person in the whole wide world, even if that whole wide world consisted of only the twelve-mile ride between Borden and New Albany, Indiana. Borden had been my home since my birth, May 29, 1842.

We were guiding the last cow in when my dad turned to me with a deep concern in his eyes and said, "Melody, we need to talk." He raked his long, thick fingers through his soaking wet hair, shaking the excess water from his hands. "It's about Lydia."

Lydia Spencer was our neighbor's teenage daughter, just a year or two older than me, though

I was much more mature than she was. Her parents owned the chicken farm two miles up the road. We had been spending a lot of time together recently, and had become rather close. It was lonely being an only child, and Lydia's company was welcome.

"What is it, Father?" I asked, a bit confused as I anticipated his response.

The rain pummeling the roof of the barn was the only sound slicing through his silence. His face was pained, and he fidgeted and seemed uncomfortable in his own skin over the conversation he was about to have with his teenage daughter. "Well, I know you've been spending a lot of time together recently and…" He paused for a moment before finding the courage to go on. "I've noticed how close you've become." I stood there quietly, not sure what he was going to say next. Then, "I want you to stay away from her."

My eyes widened at the very thought. I had become accustomed to seeing the pretty girl with the long, red hair on an almost daily basis. I didn't quite understand my own feelings. My stomach fluttered and my palms got sweaty whenever she was around. Whatever these feelings were, I knew they made me feel good.

"But Father, why?" My eyes pleaded with him to take back what he said.

"Sit down, Melody." He gestured toward an overturned bucket that we used to milk the cows, and I sat down. My attention was given completely to him as he started. "When your beautiful mother died giving birth to you, it was both the worst and best day of my life. Your mother was my world, and I have yet to stop reeling over the loss of her. Had it not been for you, I may not be walking this earth as I do today. You were a part of her, and you needed me."

I had no idea where he was headed with this, but I listened intently. "It was just me, and I didn't know how to raise a child on my own, let alone raise a girl. I cursed God for not giving me a son. A boy I could raise to be a man. But a girl…" He paused once more, seeming to have forgotten he was talking to me altogether. His gaze roamed the extent of the barn before bringing his attention back to me. "I didn't know how to raise a girl, so putting you in britches instead of dresses seemed easier. Your mother would never have approved, but she left me to raise you by myself."

It was true. My father had me in britches since I could remember. His brother, my uncle Conrad, and his wife, Lucinda, had made the 190-mile trek from Marion to Borden when I was a toddler. They were both horrified to see this tiny, curly haired girl dressed like a boy. Aunt Lucinda immediately bought suitable dresses for me. But much to her dismay, I cried my little eyes out and stomped my feet every time she put one on me.

My father eventually realized that he could only use the excuse of me doing men's work on the farm to keep me in britches for so long. The only time I was forced to wear a dress was when we went into town for supplies, or when he took me to church. I was thankful that church wasn't an every-Sunday occurrence. He was a God-fearing man, but he was a tired man. At least that's what he would say to me.

It was mostly just us who ran our dairy farm. With the assistance of a few hands a few times a week, we did all right, and were able to get by with the things we needed to survive. We cultivated a section of land to grow all sorts of fruit and vegetables, and we sustained ourselves on this food all year. We kept pigs and chickens as well. My uncle Lester and a couple other cousins of my father butchered hogs in November or December, so as to limit spoilage. The meat was stored in a smokehouse all winter.

He was a tired man indeed. Not only did my father have to maintain the farm and hands that helped out, he kept our home. He left the cleaning to me, and he cooked until I learned. Most of his free time was spent being my teacher. He never sent me to school, instead choosing to school me at home. He taught me what he thought was necessary in life: reading, writing, arithmetic, and how to be self-sufficient. He never wanted me to have to depend on a man to survive. Somehow, I think he knew from when I was a very young age that I was different than most girls. He was preparing me for an unknown future.

"You're growing and developing at a speed beyond my comprehension," he admitted, and added, "And Lydia, although she's a nice girl, has been coming around and spending a lot of time with you. I realize you're at an age where boys are going to start courting you."

I was even more confused by his words. My face scrunched up in total distaste. "I don't like boys," I said as plainly as possible, never afraid to confide in my father yet not wanting to disappoint him.

"Maybe it's time to start wearing some dresses. Boys like girls that wear dresses."

"But I don't like boys, Father," I reiterated, raising my voice a little too loudly for his liking.

"Melody, if you don't like boys, you can't like girls either. It's not acceptable."

"I don't like girls," I said, leaning back, unsure of my own words.

"I've seen the way you and Lydia look at each other. It needs to stop. Your life will be ruined." He paced the length of the barn, the hay breaking and flattening below his feet. On his way back, he stopped dead in his tracks, bent down to my level, and directly said, "No matter how much you think you care for a lady, you must never lay your hands on her. Do you understand?"

I looked at him, dumbfounded, and replied, "No, Father, I don't."

"Romantic love…romantic love can only be felt between a man and a woman. Whatever romantic feelings you think you have toward Lydia, you must never act on them. If you won't take a man, you'll be a spinster your whole life. Are you all right with that?"

I frowned, unhappy about even having this kind of talk. He kept going, though. "Society is unforgiving, Melody, and unwilling to overlook such abnormalities of the heart. It's perverse. Do you understand?"

Again, he waited for me to say something in return to his wisdom. Rather than go on with this conversation any longer, I simply nodded yes.

❧❧❧❧

I only saw Lydia once more, when my father brought me to church. Awkwardly wearing a dreaded dress, I sat in the pew with him and searched the crowd of parishioners to find her. When my gaze finally fell on her, she was sitting calmly with her parents, her yellow dress flowing freely over the bench and her hands folded in her lap. Always the proper girl. I finally gained her attention, but when I did, she quickly averted her eyes. Several times she lifted her gaze from the ground, only to find me still focused on her. The last time she looked up, our eyes locked for a moment, and she smiled, even as her mother shot me a look of pure disgust and leaned into her husband's ear to whisper something. I'm sure it was about me. She abruptly took her daughter's hand and hurried both Lydia and her husband out the door, leaving Mass early.

Although I was as heartbroken as a fifteen-year-old girl could be, I held my head high and listened to the rest of the preacher's sermon. In that instance, I realized and sorrowfully accepted that my life would be a lonely one. I wasn't fit to be with a man, even if a man did court me. I knew I would have absolutely no interest. I would become the spinster my father said I would become.

Returning home from church that day, I set out to work hard and hone the skills my father had taught me. It was bad enough coping with the loss of my friend Lydia, but trying to handle my feelings for girls, feelings that grew stronger every day, was something I had to work on. I knew I had to hide those feelings and wear a mask, so to speak. It wouldn't be easy, but it was necessary.

Luckily, I had a few abilities that would help reinforce the feminine façade. Of all the skills my father taught me, sewing was the one chore he hated most, and he insisted that I learn it and learn it well. I got so good at it that his bachelor friends began bringing their clothes to me for tailoring and their socks for mending. Even some of his married friends came to me to tailor their suits. By the time I was nineteen, their wives were impressed with my work as well. Some of them even began coming to me for my services. I had enough work by that time, so I started charging money for my talents. The second skill he taught me was how to cut his hair. That one took a little more practice, but after many, many bad haircuts I finally got the hang of it. I didn't know then how important a craft it would turn out to be later in my life.

※ ※ ※ ※

We usually rode into town about once a month to replenish supplies, and although we had just been to town a couple of weeks ago, I was in desperate need of a few spools of thread. The trotting of the steeds leading our buggy kicked up rocks and gravel as we rode down the rugged dirt road and through the center of town. We passed by the milliner's store, a cigar shop, and then the saloon before coming to a halt in front of Perkins General Store.

My dad hopped out of the buggy and tied the horses to a hitching post. "Go get what you need. I'll be across the way in the cigar shop," he said as he walked one way and I walked the other.

I opened the front door of the store and entered. The room was dimly lit, and the potbelly stove, though not in use, was in the way. The dampness made for a musty smell, and with it a sneeze from me.

"God bless you, Melody Coffield," I heard from behind the counter. Violet looked up from the cash register at me, a big smile adorning her lovely face. She pulled the handle, and the cash drawer popped out from underneath. Her eye contact sent butterflies rushing and tumbling through my stomach.

I felt my cheeks flush. "Thank you, Violet Perkins."

I browsed the store, sifting through boxes and barrels of goods crammed together on the floor beneath some shelves. I acted as though I was perusing, when in fact I knew the entire time exactly what I needed and where it was located. Every time I came into the store, I couldn't help but take my time accumulating my purchases. Anything to spend as much time as I could with the bewitchingly beautiful Violet. Granted, I knew to keep my facial expressions plain, to not give up my feelings through my eyes or smile, but each time I stole a glance at her, my heart swelled and my throat became dry, as if it were stuffed with cotton.

Her features were dainty and her wrists small as I watched her reach up onto a shelf too high for her to get to without a step stool. Her low-cut bodice accentuated the milky apricot color of her skin. The fullness of her breasts dared to challenge the confines of her dark green dress. Tiny curling tendrils escaped the heavy silken mass of hair that was as black as a starless night. Her facial bones were delicately carved, her lips full, but the most accosting feature on her were her sparkling eyes, bluer than the summer sky. The infectious grin on her face always set the tone for our brief encounters.

People that roamed the small store conversed with each other openly about their opinions of our new president and the onset of a civil war with our brethren to the south. In our great state of Indiana, people seemed to be torn on the subject of slavery, and whether new states entering the Union were to be slave or free. I didn't really have an opinion one way or the other. I hadn't known any negroes. They just weren't around where I was from. The only time I'd ever seen negroes was in New Albany, and they were only passing through with their masters on the way to the bigger city of Indianapolis. If asked to ponder on the issue and give an opinion one way or the other, I didn't think it proper, or Godly, to enslave another human being. To call another person chattel was ill will of evil men. If I'd been a man and had to pick a side to fight for, well, quite frankly, I would have fought for the North. I knew a couple of boys from out in the sticks who were willing to take up arms with them boys in the South, but I didn't think I could.

Amidst the contrary bickering between the townsfolk, Violet smoothly made her way over to me as I chose several spools of thread. Her father rung people up on the cash register, keeping an eye on his daughter, who was just a year older than me. I had known her since we were children, meeting in this store and sharing in the holy gospel on Sundays. Violet had several suitors wishing to court her over the past year, but showed no interest in any, much to her parents' chagrin. They had been encouraging her to marry since she was sixteen, wanting her to have her own life with a husband and children. Her brothers and sisters were already married and had moved from the family homestead, starting their own lives and families. But Violet remained at home, helping out with the family business instead.

"Hi, Melody." She spoke softly to me, her eyes flirting with me, and I struggled to keep my wits about me.

"Hi, Violet," I replied, suddenly aware of the stares we were getting even as we simply greeted one another.

Although I wore a dress when I wasn't at the

farm, the townspeople had their suspicions about me. They were all aware of the way my father had raised me and disagreed strongly with his childrearing ways. They insisted that he had ruined me from birth. I never did get used to the stares or whispers. It was uncomfortable to say the least, and standing here talking to a beautiful young woman, not yet married and gazing at me with a gleam in her eye, made the others gawk at us as they peered up from their own conversations to invade ours.

"I missed you the last time you and your father were here. I was away visiting family in Indianapolis. How have you been?" she asked, uncaring of the continued eavesdropping surrounding us.

"I've been well. Caring for the farm as always, and becoming quite the tailor." I gestured at the threads in front of me, and continued. "How was the city? Did you get to visit with your uncle Alexander?" I asked because I knew he was her favorite of her many uncles.

"Sadly, I did not. He's leading the organization and training of Union troops there, says he has a calling to do his duty." She was clearly glum over his absence, but understood he needed to do what a man does in honor of his country.

"God be with him and this country," I said, afraid for what the future held for our great nation.

"And what about you?" Violet asked. "I understand you have people from all over town coming to you for tailoring and mending of garments. Maybe you could teach me sometime. I've never been so good at it, and—"

"Violet, that's enough fraternizing with the customers. Get to your chores now," her father said sternly, abruptly breaking up our already short conversation.

She glanced at her father, and then back at me, rolling her eyes as she did so. "I guess I'll see you next time you come to town. You have my address, so I don't know why you never write to me."

"I'm not so good with words, Violet. I would only sound foolish, and I don't like to sound foolish."

My eyes shied away from the intense gaze she had on me, before her father once more, and with greater bravado, snapped, "Violet! Now."

Needing no other commands, she turned from him and bid me farewell. "See you again, Melody Coffield. Take care." She gave a half wink and scurried out the back door, leaving me standing there empty in her wake. I had hoped to spend a little more time with her today, even under the scrutiny of her father's ever-watchful eye, but it was not to be. I picked up the few remaining items I needed and approached the register. Her father rang up my purchases, but in between each item he took a gander at me, trying to figure me out. My father had taught me well, and I knew to wear a poker face. Our transaction and awkward interaction ended, and I was thankful to get away from him and out the door.

My father was already waiting in the buggy. I hopped in and put my sack of merchandise in the back. When I lifted my head and looked at my father, he had a cigar in his mouth, lit and puffing away. "You ready?" he asked. I nodded my head, and he directed the horses to trod back down the center of town, taking the same route back that we had taken here.

☙☙☙☙

Fall soon came to a close, and while winter came

on with such force, my father fell ill. I could barely get him up most mornings, and work was almost unheard of. He spent most days sitting in the kitchen huddled up as closely as he could to the potbelly stove in the center of the room. I couldn't cover him in enough blankets to keep him warm. But nighttime was the worst. He sweat so badly that I would soak a wash rag in a bucket of water and dab his forehead for any relief possible. The cough seemed to get worse by the day.

Each new sunrise brought with it colder and colder temperatures, and maintaining my farm duties became impossible. My father was my right arm on the farm, and I was his. Without him, I couldn't keep up. I needed reinforcements, and I needed them quickly. Father wasn't getting better, and I needed help with him, too. I sent word to Uncle Lester and Aunt Betty, who lived in a neighboring town, to come as soon as they could.

Lester finally arrived after the new year, but without Aunt Betty. She was to stay and look after the home and their children. As long as he could make the fifteen-mile trek back and forth every so often to see them, he would stay as long as I needed. He slept on a feather mattress in the front room of our house, since bunking with my father was out of the question for fear of contamination.

The farm started to function once again, but my father's health was deteriorating. My uncle finally convinced me to contact the local doctor in Borden. Dr. Evans took the five-mile ride from town, and when he saw the condition of my father, he shook his head back and forth, almost as if he knew right away what was wrong with him. He examined him anyway, coming to the same conclusion he no doubt had silently reached when he arrived.

"Consumption," he simply said, diagnosing my father with what we all knew was a deadly disease. "Best he can do is rest, eat well, and get outside in the fresh air to exercise some."

"I can barely get him out of bed most days, Dr. Evans. How am I going to get him to exercise?"

"Well, at least get him outside in the fresh air. The air is good for his lungs."

"I'm having a hard time caring for him by myself. Uncle Lester is a big help with the farm, but caring for him…" I nodded toward my dad, curled up in a ball under a blanket in his bed. "I need more help."

"I'll ask my niece, Violet, if she wouldn't mind helping out with the cooking and cleaning for a bit. I'll get back to you when I speak with her."

"Wait…who?"

"My niece, Violet. I believe you know her from the general store in town, yes?"

"Oh, um, yes. Yes, I do." I had thought about Violet often since our last encounter, but I hadn't seen her since the end of November, when my father had begun to get sick and money was scarce.

"Well, then, I shall send for her at once. I'm sure it would be her pleasure, being she hasn't married yet." He snickered, grabbed for his overcoat, and left through the front door.

The anticipation of seeing Violet again ran rampantly through my thoughts. Her sweet face and adoring smile were welcome visions in my mind. Winter had been cold and dreary, bringing with it a loneliness I had never felt. I prayed for better days ahead and wished for spring to come early this year.

Chapter Two

I rode the extent of the 200 acres of farmland and woods atop my favorite red dun quarter horse, Crimson. It was almost dusk, and the chill in the air was crisp. The clouds in the sky suggested possible snowfall. We traversed through the grove, trotting around trees with the fallen brown leaves of winter crunching under the hooves of my steed. When we came into a clearing, I brought him up to a gallop. I needed to expend some energy, energy that wasn't from work but from concern. My thoughts were all of my father. Coping with his illness hadn't been easy, and recognizing that he might never get better was painful to my heart. I was doing the best I could, but it was all up to God now, and I would have to accept whatever the outcome. It was simple to say, but in reality my heart couldn't deal with the possible death of the dearest person in my life.

On the last leg of our journey, Crimson's stride quickened with the lash of my riding crop to his hide as he dashed toward home. I held on to the reins while the cold wind whipped over my face. As I approached the house, I noticed a horse and carriage coming up the drive, and I raced in that direction to meet whoever had arrived. The carriage came to a halt and the driver got down to open the door for the passenger inside. Crimson stalled immediately in front, but before I could get down, the mystery visitor appeared from within. My eyes laid vision to the lovely Violet as the driver offered his hand to help her down.

Her dark blue dress, with its pagoda sleeves, included a high neckline and collar. Draped over her shoulders was a chestnut-colored wool cape with black trim braiding and fringe, tied at her neck. She was a sight for sore eyes. My internal battle began as I admired the curves of her hips where the dress flared into a bell. I quickly shook the perverted thoughts from my head and climbed down from my horse.

"Good evening, Violet. I'm surprised to see you." I grabbed her travel trunk from her driver.

"Miss, that's heavy. I should take that from you." He reached to take it back.

"Leave it. I can manage," I snapped, more than capable of carrying the heavy item.

"It's all right, Henry. You may leave us now," Violet said, dismissing him.

He shrugged his shoulders, and replied, "Suit yourself, miss." He took his leave, climbed up in the driver's seat, and yelled, "HA!" giving the reins a good shake and setting the horses into motion.

As he disappeared down the drive, Violet turned to me and asked, "Why are you surprised? Uncle Thomas told me you were expecting me."

She was speaking of Dr. Evans. "Yes, he did say he would send for you, but truthfully speaking, I didn't think your father would allow it."

"Well, being as truthful as I can with you, he wasn't happy about it." She walked toward the steps to the porch. "He was worried at first, you know, about my reputation, but I assured him I was only coming to help care for your dear ill father."

I didn't have to ask why he was worried. I knew.

And she knew I knew. We were comfortable enough with each other that she felt free to speak, even if the subject was uneasy for me. We both climbed the steps and went through the front door. I bent down to place the trunk on the floor, but when I stood up, she was standing close to me. A little too close. The long lashes of her startling blue eyes batted at me as her gaze ran the length of my body.

I don't know what she saw in me that made her look at me with want. I was dressed in a man's blouse shirt, trousers, and muddy boots that came up to my knees. A black slouch hat covered my long, light brown curls that were tucked underneath, and I immediately removed it in front of the lady, allowing my long hair to spill out and down my back. At nineteen years of age I had sprouted, and stood about five inches taller than she did. She looked up at me, her mouth forming into a besotted grin. For a moment, I lost myself in her trance. Involuntarily, I ran my tongue over my lips, moistening them, and found that I began to lean into her. Our faces crept closer to one another, and our lips were just mere inches from each other.

"Let me show you to your bedchamber." I abruptly stopped myself from my own wickedness. My thoughts were unclean, and I needed to regain my composure.

She seemed to snap back into the present as well, the look in her eyes changing from a soft gaze into one of sharp focus. "Yes, that will be fine." She straightened her dress at the waist and proceeded to follow me up the staircase to the two bedrooms there, my father's and mine.

We entered my room, and I placed the trunk in its resting place, then turned to her. "There are no other rooms. You'll have to sleep here with me."

"Naturally, silly girl. When I stay at my cousins', us girls have to share a bed. I'm sure I'll rest pleasantly." Again she held my gaze, and I swallowed hard, trying my best to fend off pleasures of the flesh my body so clearly told me it wanted.

"All right then. My father's in bed if you would like to check in on him. I have to finish up some sewing downstairs." I forced myself to turn from her, breaking the spell she had on me once more, and took the steps so quickly one would have thought the devil himself was chasing after me.

❧❧❧❧

That night, I stayed up as late as I could keep my eyes open. I dreaded going to bed, knowing she would be lying there. Keeping space between us was necessary. As the rest of my candles burned out, I picked up the last one to light my way up the stairs. I opened the door, giving my best efforts to not make any noise, but failing in that quest when the door creaked as it came to a stop. I closed it behind me and set the candle down. Undressing quickly, I put my men's night attire on and climbed into bed.

Her breathing was measured, and I knew she was asleep. I lay there on my back, practically on the edge of the bed, creating as much distance as I could between us. With my hands at my sides, I tried like the dickens to fall asleep, but slumber would not come easy. I was very aware of the attractive woman lying beside me. At that moment, she stirred and rolled over toward me, but I was already on the edge of the bed still attempting to keep that space. I rolled the other way, and promptly fell to the floor.

"What? Who's there?" She awoke, startled by the loud thump I created.

"It's just me, Violet," I said calmly, picking myself up off the floor and getting back into bed. "Go back to sleep." In an instant she was back in dreamland, only now in the center of the bed, on her side still facing me. I clung to the very edge of the feather mattress, feeling her knee pressed up against my hip.

❧❧❧❧

The next morning I awoke to an empty bed, feeling I hadn't slept a wink. The sun was just rising, and I was used to being the first one up in the household. So used to caring for my father, I immediately went to his bedroom. He wasn't there. I went down the stairs and rounded the bend to the dining room where I found Violet trying to get my father to eat a piece of cornbread. He did his best, but a few bites were all he could manage. As she poured tea for him, she looked up to see me pull out a chair at the table and have a seat.

"Good morning." She reached for another cup, placed it in front of me, and got to pouring tea again.

"Good morning. How did you sleep?" I asked, wondering if she had the same trouble that I had.

"I slept peacefully. There was no snoring in this house, as is usually the custom in mine." She giggled a bit, and asked, "How about you? I hope I didn't take up too much space in your bed."

"Well, maybe we can work on that. I didn't much sleep, if I did at all."

"Oh, I'm so sorry. I'll try to be more aware. I

hope I didn't impede on your personal space."

"No, no. It's okay, just something I need to get used to. I'm not used to anyone else sleeping in my bed with me." I suddenly became very aware of my father looking from me to her, and back. I could feel his apprehension, and turned to him. "Father, how are you feeling this morning? Still no appetite, I see." I pointed to the plate in front of him and the barely touched cornbread that Violet had made that morning.

"I'm not hungry, and I'm always so tired. I don't feel well at all," he replied, and pushed the plate away from him.

It was too cold to sit outside, but we helped him over to the couch in the living room and cracked the window that he sat by, allowing the cold fresh air to enter his lungs. The doctor had said it would be good for him, and I tried to make sure he received that a couple times a day. It would be better when the weather warmed up some and we could take him out to the porch. To keep it warm inside I used more wood in the potbelly stove. I sat there stoking the fire while Violet sat with my father, unafraid of the risks to her own health. She was like that, loving and caring of others. I watched as she picked up the Bible and started reading aloud to him. He seemed to enjoy it, escaping his misery even if only through the words she read.

I grabbed a piece of cornbread for myself, and as I nibbled on it and sipped my tea, I watched her. I didn't realize she noticed me until she paused between sentences to return my gaze. My stomach dropped and filled with a restless energy only she could evoke from me. The flirting we shared in together needed no words. It wasn't necessary, for her eyes told me all I needed to know. We wanted each other. There was no question.

When I pushed my chair from the table and got up, her eyes followed me from the kitchen to the living room. I did my best to avoid her beaming stare, but each time she looked from the book to me, I failed. I failed miserably. Finding it difficult to take my eyes from her, I chose to start my day. Before I left the living room, I glanced at her once more. Her telling smile compelled my legs to go weak, and I needed a moment to collect myself before heading out the door.

❧❧❧❧

It was Sunday, and chores were a little lighter than the rest of the week. Although I didn't go to church every Sunday, it was the Sabbath in any case, and we recognized it in this house. The day passed and nighttime fell. I sat in the parlor with needle and thread in hand, and made an effort to finish some work I had to get done by the next day. Violet helped my father to bed, and I thought she then would retire for the night. However, she soon returned and sat across from me, studying me as I worked. She sat there quietly, though her eyes never left me. "What is it, Violet?" I finally asked, no longer willing to listen to the silence.

"You work so hard all the time. Do you ever have any fun?"

"What do you mean? I have fun," I answered, even while I rummaged through my memories and could find none.

"Melody…"

"Violet, I'm fine with who I am. I keep myself busy, which means my mind is busy, so I can't venture to thoughts I shouldn't have."

"What thoughts? Tell me." She was persistent.

I looked at her not knowing what to say next. I had pinned myself into a corner, and now I didn't know what to do. "It's nothing I can talk about," I said, and went back to my sewing.

She stood, walked the short distance between us, and knelt down by me, placing her hand on my knee as she did. My gaze went from her eyes to her hand, and goose bumps filled my entire body. She compelled me to swallow hard, and I quickly turned my sight from her, back to my sewing task.

"Look at me," she demanded.

"I can't."

"Why not?" she asked, sounding disappointed.

"You know why."

"You think I know why."

"Violet, why are we playing this back-and-forth game?"

I finally brought my focus from my thimble and needle to her awaiting gaze. Her eyes brimmed with tenderness and passion as her hand softly grazed my thigh. "Why do your eyes behold me the way they do?" I asked, my best efforts failing.

She reached for my cheek and ran her thumb over my bottom lip. "Violet..." I whispered as I was enraptured by her touch—a touch I had never felt from anyone, man or woman. My brain didn't know how to react, but my body responded in ways unspeakable. I was suddenly paralyzed, unable to stop what was about to happen. She leaned up and placed her mouth on mine. Her lips feather-touched mine with tantalizing persuasion. I knew I should stop this, but my body wouldn't allow me to as I returned her kiss. Her mouth opened slowly and her tongue pleaded to touch mine. Again, I allowed this to happen. A dreamy intimacy built between us, a fire I didn't understand erupting between my legs.

"No," I cried as I gently separated myself from her. "This is wrong, Violet."

"No one has to know," she whispered.

"God will know." I got up from the couch and added, "In the eyes of the Lord, this is perverse and dirty." I started for the stairs, but she stopped me.

"I'm sorry. I thought you wanted to kiss me, too," she softly said, all the while her hand holding mine.

"I do, and that's why I can't." I let her hand go, climbed the steps to my sleeping chamber, and changed into my pajamas.

Soon after, I heard her come through my bedroom door. I lay there with my eyes half closed, feigning sleep. The full moon lit up the room, casting shadows in every corner. She stood in front of the window, her silhouette outlined by the nightly glow. She began to undress. I tried to avert my eyes but found that I could not. I was enraptured with unclean thoughts of the flesh. Try as I might, keeping my hands to myself was a struggle I needed to win tonight.

She pulled her dress up and over her head, then unbuttoned her corset, freeing her bosom which the moonlight traced over, giving me only a vague view of what I wished to see. Even as my guilt consumed me completely, I still could not take my eyes from her. Her bloomers came off next, and a nightgown replaced her day attire. She took the pins from her hair and allowed the mane of black silken ringlets to fall over her shoulders and down her back.

Finally, she pulled her side of the covers down and climbed into bed. No more was said or done as we lay there listening to the deafening silence in the room. The space between us became an invisible mountain, making sure the sins of the flesh stayed buried and purity remained as it should. Should I ever sleep peacefully again?

Chapter Three

In the country, war waged on as the Union troops were having a rough go of it in the east with losses at Manassas and Ball's Bluff, Virginia. However, in the western theater of the war, the Union had not only taken the surrender of Fort Henry, Tennessee, opening the door to control of the Tennessee River, but General Ulysses S. Grant had forced surrender at Fort Donelson as well. He gained a new nickname from his men: Unconditional Surrender Grant. I was both frightened and angered by the division of just about everyone I knew. Every townsperson had brothers or cousins fighting for one side or the other, and sometimes both. Families had been split up over the state of the country, and willing to die for what each believed.

Things at the farm, though, were much the same as always. It was the middle of March, and the weather was still too bitter to get my father outside. His appetite was still lacking, and it seemed the persistent cough got worse by the day. Now he was hacking up a white, thick phlegm that would nearly choke him trying to get it up. It was the most horrible thing to watch, someone you love dying right in front of you and you being completely helpless. My father was a fighter, but he was wasting away. The struggle to survive was taking every ounce of energy he had. I kept up my front, staying strong in his presence, never letting him know I was dying right alongside of him. This vibrant, able-bodied man was now a weak and frail shell of what he once was. I pitied him so.

Violet had been staying with us for several weeks now, and the tension had not dissipated. However, instead of physical affection, we chose to form a romantic friendship, never again crossing the line we had when she first arrived. When my father was resting, and after her chores and mine were finished for the day, we would sit and sew. I had plenty of tailoring work, and she didn't mind helping, insisting she had wanted to learn more about the craft. During these times, we told stories about our childhoods and our families, whether distant or near. In between fulfilling my sewing obligations, we giggled over jokes shared only between us. We got to know each other well and had a mutual admiration for one another, always knowing our boundaries. Until that one night.

After three months of residence in our home, Violet had become quite comfortable in the house. The bedroom we shared was no different. It was during these times our temptations were tested most, lying in bed side by side. And here we were again in our nightly positions. First and foremost, she was my friend, and I needed her tonight. I kept my fears and emotions about my dying father to myself, never allowing myself to feel the grief that was in my heart. But after watching him gasping for breath today as he coughed ferociously, I finally broke down. A hot tear rolled down my cheek, followed by a parade of them. I tried to choke them down, but they refused, insisting on spilling their sorrow.

I don't even know when I ended up cradled in her arms, but all at once there I was being swaddled by her. My head lay on her breasts, and her arms were wrapped tightly around me as she rocked me back and forth, comforting me as best she could. I wept for a while, unable to stop, and hating my surrender to vulnerability. It wasn't a comfortable feeling, but she was so warm and so sweet, she made her arms a safe haven for me. I sank into her, finally giving up completely.

I don't know why or what possessed me, but I slowly lifted my head, bringing my face to hers. My eyes scanned her countenance from her chin to her lips to her petite nose. Her stunning blue eyes, even in the dark, shined bright enough to light my heart. Her gaze met mine, and the force that had been doing its best to keep us apart disappeared. I leaned into her and pressed my mouth to her soft, full lips. It was different than last time. There was more emotion. We knew each other better. We cared for one another on a daily basis. It was tender and loving, and I wanted more. Such an attraction would be perilous to both our reputations, but the fires of desire had been stoked. My tongue found its way inside her mouth, intertwining with and circling around hers.

Our gentle kissing built up into a fervent passion, and I pressed forward, moving her gently onto her back. As she did, she brought me with her, pulling me on top of her. I had no idea what I was doing, having never touched anyone in an intimate way, but I knew what I wanted to do. The burning in my loins prevented me from any rational thought. The idea of burning in hell for my perverseness didn't seem to matter at this point. My lips left the comfort of hers and kissed all over her neck, tasting the saltiness of her skin. A forced hard breath came from her throat while I suckled her neck. I dragged the bottom of her nightgown up and over her breasts. For a moment, I just stared at them. Her breasts were beautiful, and as I bent down to take one into my mouth, I heard, "Melody! Violet!" It was my father. "Come quickly! Please!"

We jumped from a parallel paradise back to reality in a heartbeat. I stumbled out of the bed and toward the door with Violet right behind me. When we went into his room, he was bent over a pail, coughing and spitting up viscous, white phlegm. Along with the thick mucus was a dark color mixed in with the rest. The closer we moved toward him, the more we realized he was coughing up blood. I panicked, swearing tonight would be his last night on earth, but after some time the cough subsided enough for him to get back in bed and rest. He lay there, his eyes filled with so much pain, the transparency of his agony evident in his sunken cheeks. "I'd like to talk to Melody alone now, Violet," he said in a voice so weak it was barely audible. She left the room, closing the door behind her. I pulled up a chair by his bed and had a seat.

He had become so frail in the months since the beginning of winter. I could hardly recognize him. His hands, once so big and strong, were now feeble and wrinkled, as signs of stress appeared in different ways on his body. He reached out to me and took my hands in his. His eyes suggested a solemn conversation was about to take place. I hadn't seen that look in his eyes since the last serious talk we had when I was fifteen years of age. On the brink of turning twenty, here we were again. "Melody..." he said. I could tell he was searching for the right words during his pause, but again, he said, "Melody..."

"Father, what is it?" I asked, the anticipated subject of this conversation already making me uneasy.

"How are things between you and Violet? Are you getting along all right?"

"I guess they're fine, such as they are."

"She's been a big help around here for both of us," he admitted to me.

"She has. Maybe we should talk about this in the morning. You need your rest, Father."

"True enough, but I'm not finished yet," he said. I had started to get up, but he quickly continued. "Sit back down. I said I'm not yet finished." He gestured toward the empty chair, and I took a seat once more. I knew exactly where he was headed with this conversation, and all I wanted to do was sink into the chair in which I sat and disappear. But it was not to be. Instead, he pressed on. "I'm dying, Melody. And because I'm dying, I need you to know a few things." He took as big a breath as he could and coughed it out hard, sputtering up more phlegm, without blood this time. He readjusted his position in the bed and tried to build up the energy and strength to say what he felt needed to be said at 2:00 a.m. "When I've taken my last breath on this earth, I want you to stay true to God. No sins of the flesh, just like we talked about a few years ago. You remember, yes?"

"Of course I do, Father," I answered, fidgeting in my seat. "I know my place in this world. I know people can be cruel and that's what you've been trying to shield me from my whole life. I've always done what you've asked of me." Even as I said it, all the while I was thinking about what just took place in my bedchamber, feeling guiltier with each passing minute.

"Very well then. Now, about the farm…"

"The farm? What about the farm?"

"Well, when I'm gone, this farm will be passed down to you."

"No, I don't want it. How in the world would I ever take care of this place? It's too much for one person. Uncle Lester can barely do half the work you used to do."

"What do you mean, you don't want the farm? Missy, you listen and you listen good. I didn't work my whole life, blood, sweat, and tears, for you to just walk away. This is your life here."

All at once, the very thought of this farm and this town being my life was not at all what I wanted. The townsfolk stared at me as if I were some kind of freak. I knew damn well I was not. My father had always been my strength, my protector. I never worried about the looks or the whispers because my father would never let anyone hurt me. However, feeling the loss of him before he was even gone hurt so much. I finally broke down in front him, not wanting to but having no choice, the tears forcing their will upon me. I couldn't bring my eyes to his as I wept uncontrollably.

"It's okay," was all he said. I felt his hand take mine in his again. When I finally looked up at him, he was crying, too. My father, the big burly man I had always known, let loose his grief through his tears about his own eventual death. His tears made it all the more real for me. I didn't think I was going to be able to cope with his passing. He was all I'd ever known in my life. He kept me so sheltered that I wasn't sure I could live without him. And, quite frankly, I didn't know if I even wanted to. I wasn't allowed to be myself, because I wasn't normal. I didn't want a man, and I knew I was in for a solitary existence when he was gone, a future I didn't look forward to, blurred with doubt and uncertainty. I shook and shivered with fear.

He tugged at my hand, pulling me up and out of my chair and into his arms. He held on to me for dear life. "My sweet daughter." He cried into my shoulder, his sorrow and own mortality realized. "You have been my reason for living. I love you. You need to know that I love you and I will always love you, whether from here or there." He looked and pointed to the sky. "I'm always going to be with you. Right here." He touched his index finger to my heart.

"I love you, too. Please don't leave me. Please don't go. I can't go on." I choked on the tears pouring down my cheeks, begging him with all that I had.

He lifted my face to meet his eyes and told me, "You will go on, Melody. You must. It's almost time for me to go home to your mother. She's been without me for some time now."

I sat there on the side of the bed letting my father cradle me as if I were still a young child. We both needed it. I don't know that either of us felt any better about anything, but at least we had a heartfelt moment.

We sat there for some time like that, not saying a word, just holding one another. At some point he confessed he was exhausted, and I left his room, closing the door behind me and looking at the door in front of me. My door. The door that held Violet behind it. I needed to pull myself together. I wiped the remnants of my tears on the back of my hand and opened the door. When I got into bed, she was on her back and lying still. I, too, lay on my back, and although I thought she had fallen asleep, I was soon found wrong as I felt her hand on top of mine. I needed her touch, just a comforting touch. The heat of the moment from earlier had passed. We had both come to our senses during the little time I spent with my father. We slept that way the rest of the night.

Morning came swiftly. I awoke just as the sun was on the horizon. I lay on my side, and while I attempted to blink the sleep from my eyes, I recognized and felt an arm around my waist, a warm body pressed up against my back. I knew I should get up. After all, I and Uncle Lester had to milk the cows this morning and get to the market as soon as possible. But I lay there instead, soaking up the feel of her and basking in the dizzying feelings she stoked in me. She felt so good, and yet I knew it was all forbidden. It didn't make it easier just because it was forbidden. On the contrary, it made it that much harder.

Eventually, I got up, got dressed, and went downstairs to get Uncle Lester, who was already up and outside in the barn. By the time we milked the cows and were ready to go to market, Violet was up and caring for my father. The rest of her day would be spent doing household chores and cooking supper. After the day was ended and our travel finished, Uncle Lester and I came home to the aroma of freshly cooked food. We were famished, and walking into the house to a set table with boiled mutton, stewed liver, and vegetables was a welcome sight.

"Where is Father?" I asked first and foremost.

"He doesn't want to eat. I tried. He's in his room, resting," Violet answered.

The three of us sat and filled our bellies. Pudding was for dessert, but before I ate that, I went to check on my father. I peeked in through his bedroom door and saw him curled up on his side with his eyes closed. I didn't know if he was asleep or not, but I knew that it was a rarer and rarer occurrence for him to not be coughing miserably. Currently, he seemed to be resting somewhat peacefully, so I left him to it.

I returned downstairs to find that Uncle Lester had retired to the parlor and was smoking a cigar. Violet and I sat at the kitchen table and ate our pudding. Occasionally, I would look up in between bites to catch her glancing at me. I knew she was thinking of what took place last night in bed, and so was I. It was something that hadn't left my mind all day. Even as I was at the market today, her face crept from the back to the front of my mind. Maybe if we didn't talk about it, it would go away. These feelings. These yearnings. But even as we sat there, quietly eating our dessert, we longed for each other.

⁂

The evening passed, and once again it was dreaded bedtime. There was always a struggle within right before bed, knowing I wanted to feel her lips on mine again, yet knowing these were such wicked thoughts. My body awoke whenever she was near to me, and I didn't know how much more I could take. When we entered the room together, she began undressing for bed. I tried so hard to avert my eyes, but the demons within me wouldn't allow it. After taking off her dress, she unhooked her corset. As she slipped it off, she brought her gaze to me, knowing I was watching her. She slipped out of the rest of her undergarments and approached me while I stood paralyzed by her beauty.

She placed her hands on my face and caressed my cheek with her fingertips. The longing we felt for each other grew to a passion neither of us could control any longer, and she kissed me tenderly as she unbuttoned my shirt. She dragged it over my shoulders and pushed it to the floor. Her kiss sent new spirals of ecstasy through me. Unbuttoning my trousers was her next course of business, and although I knew I would burn in hell for eternity for what was about to take place, I chose to burn. I could feel her uneven breathing on my cheek as I pulled her closer.

We eased toward the bed, her lying down first and me crawling on top of her, just as I had the previous night. This time, we were naked. Flesh upon flesh. Her heart against my heart. My tired soul melted into her kiss. Her lips were warm and sweet on mine, and my appetite for her built into a frenzy I had never before felt. My defenses were not only weakened, they had become nonexistent as we crossed the forbidden line from platonic friends to romantic lovers.

Having never had this kind of physical contact with anyone before, I let her sounds guide me. I didn't know if she had any prior experience, but we took our time to explore, to arouse, to give each other pleasure. Her breasts surged at the intimacy of my touch and I took one into my mouth, my tongue tantalizing the bud which had swollen to its fullest. I explored her rosy peaks, escalating my own arousal through her soft moans.

My hand slid down her taut stomach to the swell of her hips. My own hips involuntarily jutted forward, meeting the rise of hers. I kissed each part of her body, indulging in the softness of her skin. She matched my urgency with her own lusty, unsated needs. Her hands moved magically over my breasts, encouraging me to continue my exploration. I slid my hand between her thighs, her tormented groan an invitation. I sank into her, filling her velvety tunnel and eliciting moans of pleasure from both of us. We were connected, not in perversion but in love, and I let it swallow me whole.

We knew we had to be quiet, but silence was a real challenge. Our bodies, moist from our lovemaking, writhed together. Waves of ecstasy throbbed through us, finding a tempo that bound us as one. She shattered the hard shell that I had built so carefully over the years, allowing me to love her as well as allowing her to love me. She gasped in sweet agony, reaching the apex of her bliss.

We lay there tangled in each other's bodies, tenderly kissing and caressing one another, smiling and quietly giggling. Her fingers coursed through my hair, and she looked deeply into my eyes. I couldn't control my lips as I whispered, "I love you, Violet."

Even through the dim light of the candle in the room, her smile shined like the sun. The back of her hand swept softly over my cheek, her gaze still connected to my eyes. "I love you, too, Melody." I knew this passion had to stay unseen and unknown, and as if she heard my inner thoughts herself, she added, "Our love must remain in this room. We cannot look at each other like this once we step across that threshold. You do understand, yes?"

I nodded in agreement, not saying a word, completely lost in love with her.

Chapter Four

The rooster's cock-a-doodle-doo broke through the quiet, peaceful morning, beckoning me to begin my day and my daily duties. Lying fast asleep in my arms was Violet, her ebony curls flowing over the pillow beneath her lovely head. The last thing I wanted to do was leave the confines of this room, but it was a necessity. I peeled my naked flesh from hers and got up out of bed. The sun was just on the horizon, so the room was still fairly dark as I searched for my clothes.

I stood there dressing, buttoning my shirt and pulling up my trousers. I then sat in the chair to pull up my boots, studying her as I did. She lay there so peacefully and innocent, her breathing relaxed and even. Last night had been an awakening experience for me. I felt like a different person this morning somehow. Something inside of me had changed. Each time I laid my eyes on her, my heart glowed with love. My admission was dredged from a place beyond logic and reason.

Part of me delighted in these newfound mutual feelings, and part of me knew the angst I would feel once I crossed from this room to the next, overwhelmed with reality. A reality that would never understand this. I had never known love like this—if, in fact, this was love. The harder I tried to ignore the truth, the more it persisted. What I considered to be lovemaking others would describe as carnal desire and sin. Although I began to recognize my own needs, I knew I had no choice but to stifle them.

The last thing I did was put my suspenders on, and before leaving the room I knelt beside her side of the bed. I brushed away a few strands of hair from her face and softly kissed her forehead, knowing when I walked out that door, I had to shut it all down. She stirred some and then her eyes fluttered open. Her mouth curved into an adoring smile, and I felt myself smile back. I stroked her hair, and said, "Good morning." She started to rise, but I stopped her. "It's still early. Get a little more sleep."

"A good morning it is. I am well rested, and ready to get some chores finished that I ignored yesterday." She pulled the covers back and got up.

I headed for the door, but as I reached for the doorknob a little voice inside of me said, *When you leave this room, you leave her.* I paused, turned around, and went back to her. She was just putting on her corset when I took her in my arms and kissed her hard. Abruptly, she pulled away from me, stunned, and a bit taken aback. "What was that?"

Seeing her spooked, I realized maybe I should explain myself. "I apologize, Violet. It's just that I know once I leave the bedroom today, I won't be able to do that."

She thought on my words for a second, and soon a tight smirk came over her face. Without any other words, she kissed me back just as hard, understanding we wouldn't be in one another's arms again until bedtime. It would be a long day for both of us. The sparkle in her eyes matched the sparkle in mine. There was no denying our fondness for each other.

Knowing there was work to be done, I finally broke our embrace and hastened out the door. As soon as I closed the door behind me, the air changed and thickened. I found it hard to breathe at first, and I needed to take a few deep breaths before going downstairs. By the time I became calm, my father's morning coughing had begun. I went for his door, but Violet came quickly from our bedroom. "Not to fret. I'll care for your father. You go milk the cows. I'm sure Uncle Lester is waiting patiently for you downstairs." We gave one last heartfelt look at one another, then she shooed me down the steps. By the time I reached the bottom and turned to look up, she was already in my father's bedchamber.

❧❧❧❧

Uncle Lester was in a disagreeable mood, but we got through milking the cows and settling the barrels into the back of the buggy. The horses started on their way, already knowing the familiar route to New Albany. We rode through town and entered the market, full of people purchasing their wares. Once we began selling our milk, the talk between townspeople seemed to be about two things: first, the battle at Pittsburgh Landing, Tennessee. As I understood it from listening to others, it was a Union victory, but a very slim one. The casualties were innumerable on both sides, the carnage unfathomable. Everyone swore General Grant was well on his way to destroying the Army of the Mississippi, and then on to Richmond and Lee's Army of Northern Virginia. Most of us in Borden were rooting for the North, which led to the second subject of which the townsfolk spoke:

volunteering and signing up for one of the units being organized around the state.

Men I had known my whole life were joining. Fathers, brothers, and cousins alike were signing up in droves. Principle was why men enlisted; honor was why men fought. The women encouraged the men of their families and communities to join the cause, and men that cowered to the task were demeaned as not being men. It was a chaotic time for the country. A year into this conflict and nothing was clear. Victories had come slow to the Union Army, and I asked God to show mercy on the dead and wounded. The stories had been horrific, which had stoked the fire in me to join. But alas, women were not allowed to fight. War was for men, not women. If I could have, though, I would have.

We sold all of the milk we had brought with us and made the long trek home. Work was never done, and I had a million more things to do once we got back to the farm. When we pulled up the drive, Violet was outside scrubbing garments on a washboard and hanging them to dry on the line. The weather had started to break, and even though there was a slight chill in the air, it had been getting warmer. We were nearing the end of April, and I was glad the sun would be coming up earlier so as to get more accomplished in the day.

I got down from the buggy and waited for Uncle Lester to start back to the barn. "Don't take too long. We got plenty left to do before supper," he said as he rode off in that direction.

"Right away," I shouted back at him. I looked from him to Violet, whom I had missed the whole day. "Hello," I said, trying my best to keep my face stoic.

"Hello," she replied, and went about hanging a few stockings. "How was your day? Didn't come home with any milk, did you?"

"No ma'am. Sold it all." She turned back to the washboard and more socks, and I asked, "How's my father?"

"Same condition you left him in this morning. His state is getting no better. You should go see him. He's finally settled down and he's been waiting to take a nap to see you."

By the time I got in the house, my father was fast asleep. Even in his slumber, he never looked at peace. His face was pained with illness and anguish. Still, I let him sleep. The night passed. Supper was had and everyone nested in their own space preparing for bed. I poured some water into the basin in my room and washed my face clean before undressing. Violet was just slipping out of her corset when I turned toward her. Her breasts were beautiful in the glow from the candle. She was magnetizing, enticing, even when she wasn't trying.

"Do you like what you see?"

A bright shade of red overtook my cheeks, and as embarrassed as I was, I still nodded. She came from across the room and stood directly in front of me with longing in her eyes. "I've waited all day to be with you. I know we're not supposed to, but I can't help myself when we are alone."

I moved my face close to hers and whispered in her ear, "Oh, Violet, I do love you so." Our cheeks grazed one another as I brought my lips to hers and kissed her deeply. There was no rush like there had been that morning when I hurried out the door. No, we had all night to be as close to one another as we wanted to be, free from the gaze of unforgiving would-be onlookers. Kissing led to petting, and touching led to indescribable acts on each other. I made love to her repeatedly, and would do so night after night for the next three months.

We both knew it was wrong, and we had both been raised to believe this kind of physical touch between two of the same sex was perverse and dirty, but when Violet and I made love, I didn't see it that way. There was nothing dirty about the way I felt for her, and there was nothing perverse about the way I made love to her. And I did love her. However, the struggle between God and me, internally and spiritually, was an ongoing, daily battle. It was the same for her, but we never let that stop us from doing what we were doing. I wished that God had made me a man instead of a woman. I was meant to be a man. Cursed, I was.

❧❧❧❧

I had grown accustomed to living with her. And for the most part, we kept our union a secret. We only got caught once, and as embarrassing as it was, life went on. After the few hands we had on for the day had left for the evening, Uncle Lester happened in on a scene he was not inclined to appreciate. We thought we were alone for the evening.

The hands had gone home, and Uncle Lester said he was going to a neighboring farm to have a swig of whiskey and talk politics. My uncle wasn't the most educated man in the world, but he had more schooling than my father did, being the baby of eight children. My father was number four. But my uncle had a great interest in such matters, and ridiculed

President Lincoln for his chastising of the South and their peculiar institution of slavery. He agreed with the South in respect that states should have the right to do as they wish.

However, he started drinking outside and never made it to the Johnson farm, and it was unbeknownst to him what he was about to walk in on. We broke our cardinal rule of engaging in intimacy only in the bedroom. Violet had decided to bathe in the metal tub we had in a small washroom downstairs. It took a while to fill as she fetched bucket after bucket of water. When she was finally immersed in the fragrant oil-soaked water, I saw no harm in taking a peek. My father was asleep in his room. Uncle Lester was next door. Or so I thought.

I slowly opened the door, and her head swiftly turned toward it as it creaked in motion. When she saw it was me, she smiled a shy smile but invited me to enter the small space barely able to hold one, let alone two, people. Once inside, I knelt by the tub as she washed her body. Water flowed over her in small beads as she wrung the wash rag over her shoulders. We talked about our busy days, her churning butter and me making the ride to market, and how I would be planting corn and some other vegetables for the season.

But talking became flirting, and flirting became touching, and before I knew it, I was being pulled into the tiny tub with her. We kissed and giggled, and maybe a bit too loudly, because the door flew open, hitting the wall behind it with force. Stunned, we looked to the door to see Uncle Lester there, drunk and in disbelief of what he was seeing. Violet quickly covered her breasts with her hands, and I went to scurrying and splashing to get out of the tub. He watched this whole scene unfold as he stood there frozen and confused.

I situated myself between him and Violet as my soaking wet clothes dripped water onto the floor. I ran my fingers through my hair, wringing it out. His mouth was still agape, and he had yet to say a word. "Why are you still standing there? Uncle Lester, get out." I couldn't believe my own voice, yelling at my uncle as I did. The devil took control of my tone when I repeated, "Get out. By the grace of God, take your eyes from her!"

I don't know when I became so brazen. I would normally find this type of behavior from myself most disrespecting, but he wouldn't stop staring past me to Violet, who was still naked with her arms crossed over her breasts. I could smell the liquor on his breath as he thought better of whatever ideas he had on his mind and finally turned to leave. I heard him go into the parlor where I am sure he fell onto his mattress and passed out, unconscious.

When I turned to Violet, she was getting up out of the tub. She panicked as she dried herself off. "What are we going to do?"

"Do? Nothing."

"Nothing? He just caught you in the tub with me."

"He's inebriated. He'll be lucky to remember any of what he saw tomorrow."

"Are you sure?"

"Yes. I've seen him in this state before. And if he does remember, I'll hoodwink him into thinking he didn't." I felt confident and ill at ease all at the same time. In the interim, we never broke our rule again.

And Uncle Lester, whether he remembered what happened or not, never spoke of the uncomfortable incident.

⚬⚬⚬⚬

The months Violet and I shared with each other while she helped care for my father were significant times in my life. I came to realize who I was, though I couldn't tell anyone else. I cursed the day I was born. This life was not easy for anyone, but for someone like me, a loner, a spinster, it was more than complicated. And my father's decreasing role in my life, due to illness, was both deflating and discouraging.

During our nights together, we would make love, sharing in bliss never known to either of us, only to regret our weakness when it came to the physical part of our love for one another. Yet, that room…that room was our private little hovel where no prying eyes could see. No matter what was thought by people, nothing could ever be proven without the consent of our own admittance.

Sometimes after lovemaking, we would lie in each other's arms and fantasize about what our lives would be like together if I had just been born a man. We would dream of our house and the many children we would have. Other families would be envious of our perfect love, our perfect union of hearts. And always the discussion of God, and why it didn't feel dirty when we were together, as others said it to be. It was a never-ending debate over the spiritual approval of the Lord, but it always ended in another session of lovemaking before we fell asleep into a dreamland filled with only each other. It felt like we were asleep for an hour before the rooster would crow his morning taunt to rise and begin the day.

⁂

By the end of July, the summer heat was sweltering, and my father's condition was no better. His health was deteriorating at a quick rate now, and I feared he didn't have much time left. It was a foolish fancy to even hope or pray for his survival. Death was at his door. I couldn't get over the idea of being left on this godforsaken earth without my father. Fate would have its way.

One morning, I was downstairs preparing to go out to the cows and my morning chores when I heard my father coughing upstairs. I could hear the door to my room open, and footsteps proceeded out and across the hall to his room. Muffled voices came from the second floor.

"Melody! Come quickly," Violet yelled from the landing above.

My heart sank as I went flying up the steps, taking them two at a time. I couldn't get to my father fast enough. He was bent over a pail, Violet kneeling by his side with her hand draped around and over his back. I walked around the other side of them, putting them both in my full view. When I looked down at the bucket, it was filled with blood. There was no phlegm this time, only dark clots, big chunks of blood that had been spewed from his lungs. A rattle could be heard from within his chest. I had never heard the sounds that came from him—the sounds of approaching, imminent death.

He pushed himself onto his bed and lay on his

back. Each breath he took was painstaking labor. If he wasn't struggling for breath, he was coughing and choking on blood. Violet wiped the blood from the corners of his mouth and sat upon the bed by his side. I stroked his hair as tears filled my eyes but would not spill. I took his hand in my other, and he clutched it fiercely. The fear in his eyes was too much to stand. "Daddy, I love you. It's okay. It's okay to go home," I whispered, giving him permission to let go. "Tell Mommy I love her." His body fell limp, the coughing ceased. His eyes remained open, but he was gone.

The tears that refused to fall in front of him let loose like a river now. I laid my head on his chest and cried as if I were five years old. Deep sobs rang from inside of me as I held his empty vessel within my arms. A wave of despair spread throughout my body as my shaking hands closed his eyes. More tears came, venting the agony of my loss. I felt Violet's hand rubbing my back. When I began to choke on the very tears that grieved my father, she took me in her arms and allowed me to break down completely. I sank into the security of her loving arms and wept the death of the only man I had ever loved.

Chapter Five

We buried my father next to my mother on the family farm. I had a small but respectful service for him. There were some family, some townsfolk, and a few of his acquaintances present, Violet's parents included. When the casket was lowered into the ground and people who came to pay their respects began to depart, I noticed Violet's father speaking to her. He always wore an intense look on his face whenever I was around, and today was no different as he ended their brief conversation, pointedly glared at me, and helped Violet's mother into the carriage. Violet went into the house and I sat on the ground at my father's grave. I grabbed one of the flowers that had been placed there for him and inhaled the sweet fragrance from its bud. Looking to the sky, I searched for answers that weren't there.

When night fell and grief and despair filled my heart, Violet warmed and comforted me in her embrace. She was the one bright light in my life. I curled into her. Our bodies were wrapped around one another as she rocked me back and forth, stroking my hair. I felt safe in her arms. I felt like an orphan, without a mother or a father, but I had her. My lover, my friend, my confidante. The only other soul on this earth to truly know my own soul. How I loved her so, but those feelings were soon to be left dead.

When I awoke in the morning, she was packing

her things into her travel trunk, the same trunk she had arrived with. I rubbed my eyes to better adjust to the darkness still enveloping the room with just a hint of light. "Violet, what are you doing?" I asked, still trying to wake to the new day.

"My father is coming to pick me up."

"Pick you up? Where are you going?"

"Home, of course."

"But Violet…" I quickly arose from the bed and scampered across the room to stop her. "I thought this was your home." I reached for the garments she held in her hand.

"Why would you think this was my home?" She shook the garment from my hand, folded it, and packed it away.

"Violet." I reached for her shoulder and turned her around to face me. "I thought you loved me."

She stopped what she was doing, took my hands in hers, and looked me in my eyes. "I do love you, Melody. I don't think I shall ever love anyone the way I love you, but I must go. I was here only to help care for your father, and now that he is passed, I must go home. My father told me after the service he would have it no other way. He says I have to protect my name and reputation. My life would be ruined if I stayed here with you, and for appearance's sake, I must go home."

"I can't believe you're leaving me," I said dejectedly as she turned from me, treading a path on my floor toward the door. Before she could leave, I dashed across the room and twirled her back around. "My father just died. Please don't go!"

"I have to," she said, opened the door, and looked at me once more. Her fingertips traced the outline of my lips, feeling all that we felt for each other. She leaned her forehead on mine and kissed me softly, before saying, "I'll never forget you."

I could hear the faint sound of hooves galloping up the driveway as she dragged her trunk down the steps, a clunking sound coming with each step it fell upon. The sound of it scraping across the floor and out the door was the last of it. A lump formed in my throat, and I found it nearly impossible to swallow. I could not stop the tears that fell helplessly down my face. My heart was breaking, and the emptiness that accompanied that feeling was tremendous. I could hardly withstand the pain.

I peeked out the window and saw her father placing the trunk in the back of the buggy. He helped her up and into her seat, and went around the other side to get in. Before he shook the reins for the horses to go ahead, he caught me out of the corner of his eye. He looked up at the window and locked eyes with me, a look of disgust coming over his face. It was the same look he gave me when I perused his store, waiting for the opportunity to converse with his daughter, much to his dismay. He turned back to his horses, and gave a yell, "HA! Gitte up!" They left in a hurry, never looking back, and soon they were out of my sight.

I was alone. I was truly alone. Everyone I loved had left. A whirlwind of confusion and despair overtook me, and I leaned my back against the wall, slowly sliding down until I was in a crouched position. I hung my face in the palm of my hands and wept my pain. This crushing pain squeezed and choked the life from my heart, and my spirit was broken. What kind of life would mine be now? I glanced upward and begged my father, "What am I to do now?" My eyes dumped torrents of tears upon my cheeks. "What's to become of me?"

Every thought that occupied my mind from that day forward was the loss of my father and the loss of the love of my life. Daily chores and activities were filled with a melancholy attitude which anyone around me could feel. It didn't take much but to look at me. "You're pathetic," my Uncle Lester said to me on more than one occasion, as he was still helping out with the farm until I could figure out what I wanted to do. He tried to persuade me to follow a traditional path. "You have this farm that operates quite smoothly with just a little help. Will you please consider taking a husband?"

"Uncle Lester, I am more than sufficient enough to take care of myself."

"But it would be easier for you," he suggested. "If you did."

"It's out of the question."

❧❧❧❧

In the days that followed my father and Violet's departure from my life, Uncle Lester and I continued to go to the market with our fresh milk. New Albany was taking on a different life all of its own. The streets were filled with men newly enlisted into the Army. One company that was on its way to being mustered into service was parading down the street on their way to board a train headed southward from here. The community showed its support by hanging bunting on their stoops, and the women presented flags to represent the colors of the company. Young soldiers waited their turn to be kissed by pretty girls as they boarded the train. It was a real to-do.

Oh, how I wished I were a man right now; to board that train to parts unknown was a dream. Anything to escape the sorrow that had beseeched my life. I watched as the men cheered and sang songs. After all were aboard, they waved their hats in the air and bid the crowd of well-wishers adieu. The train's horn gave a boisterous sound. The steam from the engine shot up in a dark cloud, moving swiftly as the train chugged down the track.

My mind was shaken loose from the scene by Uncle Lester. "Melody," he exclaimed.

"Yes? Oh, I do apologize. My attention was elsewhere."

"Well, let's get to filling these bottles with milk. Come now," he said.

I gave one last look down the tracks, scanned the rest of the town and the people in it, and finally brought my attention back to our task at hand. He held the bottles while I filled them with much-needed white cream. Even as I tried to shake the excitement of the boys in blue taking to fight against their own relatives in many cases, the talk of the townspeople was all about the war. There was no escaping it. The newspapers reported no movement of troops in the East under General McClellan. President Lincoln wanted him to move on the South, but the General seemed to only train the soldiers, never giving them the chance to put that training to good use in the form of battle. When finally pressed to within removal of his command, he failed horribly in his raid up the peninsula in Virginia.

I listened intently to various people talking amongst themselves as they purchased their wares from different merchants. "My son is joining next week. When he heard his cousin was signing up, he didn't want to get left behind," one woman said to another as they picked through some fruit across the way from our barrels of milk. An old man with a haggard face told someone else, "My grandson was about to get married. Now he's rushed off to fight the Rebels. What's come of this country?"

"Melody, you're drifting again, dear," I heard my uncle say behind me. "Cap that bottle and fetch another. Come on, now."

"Yes. Of course," I said, retrieving another empty bottle and handing it to him. He placed it under the spigot of the barrel, but my mind was adrift again as I held the handle of the spigot down. I never saw the bottle fill to the brim until it was spilling over and splashing onto his hands.

"That's it. Where is your mind, girl?" he shouted, shaking his hands of the liquid. "Stop this aloofness at once. Let's complete our business for the day and return home."

The hours passed, and I tried to stay present with Uncle Lester as best I could in the state I was in, but still I listened. I absorbed all that the townsfolk had to say about the war and the boys in blue. We finally sold all our milk, and headed home for the day.

When night fell, my uncle retired for the night. I knew he wouldn't be able to stay forever, and I knew he wanted me to make some kind of decision about the farm. If I wasn't going to get married, he wanted me to move in with him and his family. But I knew Aunt Betty wouldn't be happy with that arrangement, having never been able to make conversation with me. Her awkwardness around me was evident whenever she was at the farm and observed my form of dress. The other option was to keep the farm, but I would have to hire some full-time hands to keep it running. I wasn't thrilled with any of these choices.

With each passing day, the void of not having my father in my life cut me like a knife. Having been abandoned by Violet was like having that same knife stab my chest repeatedly and deeply, aiming for the gaping hole where my heart had once beat. I led a lonely existence, and the lows had gotten to me in a way that made self-inflicted death seem imminent and, sadly, welcome. I didn't know how much longer I could live like this. It was all too much.

❧ ❧ ❧ ❧

At the end of August, I made the monthly trek into town. I needed supplies, and the general store was where I needed to get them. I was a bit anxious, as this would be the first time I would see Violet since she had left me a month ago. When I entered the store, her father's glare was the first thing to greet me. His eyes narrowed, and his scowl was all I needed to realize I was not welcome. However, I needed the items I needed, and whether I saw Violet or not, I couldn't leave until I had them. Part of me didn't even care to see her, the part of me that was still filled with so much pain. The other part of me missed her so much that seeing her felt necessary.

I picked up some honey and dried beans, and put them in my sack. Then I made my way over to the table filled with baskets of spools of thread and picked through them.

"Hi, Melody," I heard from behind me. It was

her. My heart quickly jammed in my throat, knowing the beautiful hum of her voice so well.

I turned toward her, aiming to speak to her as if she didn't matter, but when my eyes met hers it was all I could do to get words to come out of my mouth. Her beauty mesmerized me so, and images of our time spent together flickered through my mind. Images of the way her lips felt on mine, and how loved I felt when I was in her arms.

"Hi, Violet." I finally formed words.

If I didn't know what to say to her, she surely seemed to feel the same. I wanted to tell her how much I missed her, but I knew that was out of the question while surrounded by so many onlookers. She, on the other hand, always being braver than I was in situations of discomfort, whispered softly, "I think about you all the time." Her eyes roved the room, making sure no one was in earshot of her. Her words melted my core into a puddle of pathetic adoration for her, but just as I was about to respond, a young man I had never met before came up behind her and put his hands on her waist.

"Dear heart, your father requests your presence in the upstairs living area."

"At once." She nodded.

As he stepped away, I asked out of sheer curiosity, "Who is he?"

He looked at her the way I looked at her, and in the pit of my stomach I knew what she was about to tell me. Her eyes lent a painful look of sadness, almost mourning the death of our love, as she confessed to me: "I'm to marry him."

Her words stung as badly as if she had struck me across the cheek. They sliced through me, shredding what little was left of my love for her. "No," I said, shaking my head back and forth while forbidding the tears that threatened to fall. I stepped back from her, wondering who this person was before me. Surely, she could not be the same Violet who had lain in my arms, vowing her love to me behind closed doors. I guess she had the right to a normal life that society could accept, but it broke my heart that I couldn't give that to her. Had I only been a man… But I wasn't, and I was completely broken.

"Melody," she whispered, clearly wanting to comfort me but knowing she could not. She slowly stepped away from me and bid me good-bye. "I'm sorry."

She turned quickly then, and raced toward the stairs that led to their family's residence. As she flew past her betrothed, he looked over at me. Upon seeing my upset countenance, confusion spread across his face, inviting suspicion of what he could not possibly realize. Our eyes connected, and even though I made an effort to go blank in my expression, I could not help but glare at him in an evil way. The very thought of him touching her, putting his hands places that I had, was agonizing, and the jealousy I felt made me abhor not only him, but myself as well. I needed to gather my things and leave in a hurry.

I shuffled through the other patrons to the line at the cash register and placed the contents of my sack onto the counter. Lucid, my mind was not, and I stared at the things Violet's mother rung up. Something came over me when I began directing her to load the sack with ammunition for my .577 Enfield musket rifle. She looked up from the register, her mouth agape and stunned, surely wondering what I, a woman, wanted with ammunition. I scared her further when I asked to dump a bunch of cartridges in as well.

"What do you want with these things, Melody?" she asked, never being one to mind her business.

"Never you mind, ma'am," I answered, doing my best to remain respectful but continuing nonetheless. "Just put them in the sack."

She did as I instructed and gave me my total due. I handed her payment, scooped up my sack, gave her one last glance, and said, "Good day."

I had the ride home to think about it, this idea that had arisen in my head and was still developing. As I pulled up the drive and scanned the farm with its valleys and hills, its woods and its clearings, I couldn't help but think about my father. I couldn't help but wonder what he would think of what I thought was a scathingly brilliant idea. I almost believed he would agree with my newly thought-out plan. He would be concerned but he would understand, knowing what he'd known since I was a small girl.

I walked into the house, poured the contents of the sack onto the table, and immediately took the ammunition and cartridges. I fetched my musket and walked briskly back outside. A sharpshooter I was not, but I set out to practicing by setting up different targets around the farm. Already eaten corncobs were most abundant, so they tended to be my favorite props.

❦ ❦ ❦ ❦

Day after day, I practiced loading the musket and firing it as fast as I could. I had gotten pretty good at loading at a quick speed, but accuracy in shooting still came slow. Uncle Lester watched from a distance, puzzled, like for the life of him he couldn't figure out what I was up to. He surely thought his niece had lost her mind altogether. But I couldn't think about him. I had to get better.

Each time I looked up to my bedroom window, I imagined Violet undressing. But my yearning turned to fury as I ripped the cartridge with my teeth, poured the powder into the muzzle, and rammed the ball and powder to the breech of the barrel with the ramrod. I primed the weapon using a percussion cap, then cocked, aimed, and fired the weapon. Smoke rose from the power of the shot, and I walked the distance to the cob I had placed upright on a barrel. When I examined the cob, I noticed a clean hole right through the center. A smile came over my face, and I knew it was time.

I ran to the house, swung the screen door open, and continued inside. I rummaged through the house searching for the scissors I used to cut my father's hair. When I finally found them, I rushed to the mirror and took off my slouch hat. I looked at myself for a second. My long, brown curls hung down my back and around my shoulders. My eyes. There was something about my eyes. No feeling seemed to be left there. Did I even have a soul anymore? My heart had been trodden, and without my father to help mend me, it was time to branch out on my own.

I combed a swath of hair through my fingers, and with the other hand took aim with the scissors and cut through it, letting the long strands fall to the floor. Once more I looked at myself, then took another bunch of hair and snipped it off. I cut it so short one couldn't tell I had curls anymore. When it was all said and done, I donned a short style of men's hair. I looked like a teenage boy, but that was a start.

With my men's hair and men's clothing that I wore on the farm, my likeness was that of a man. I took my blouse off and bound my breasts with cloth bandages, pressing them as close to my body as I could. Then I put the shirt back on and looked in the mirror again. It was complete. The decision had been made. I no longer wanted the farm, not without my father. Moving in with Uncle Lester just wasn't an option. I wanted a new start, a new beginning.

I sat at the kitchen table with pen and paper. Dipping the head of the pen into the inkwell, I began writing.

Dear Uncle Lester,

I pray this correspondence finds you well and in good spirits. Do sell the farm and hold the proceeds for me. This is my final decision as I've decided to venture out on my own. Please don't concern yourself with worry for me. I will be fine. You need not ask any questions. You only need stay in touch with me when I write. Communications may be cut off for a while, but will resume once I've found my final destination. I'm joining the Army.

I remain your faithful niece,
Melody Ann Coffield

Chapter Six

The next morning, I strapped my bosom down, dressed in my best men's attire, grabbed my musket, and climbed astride Crimson for the long ride to New Albany. The sun was shining on this warm September day, and fall would be soon approaching. I looked around, knowing this would be the last time I would see the old homestead. I reminisced over memories of my father and me. All that he taught me would not be in vain. I was about to embark on an unknown journey full of uncertainties and unforeseeable risks, but he had taught me all I knew of survival. I was confident, something I hadn't been since Violet left.

I would start a new life in the United States Army and never look back. No more emotions I couldn't control. No more hurt over my odd feelings. No, this spinster was about to live the rest of her life as a man, as long as I wasn't detected. Caution and secrecy would become the priority of the day, every day. Living as a woman was not for me. So many restrictions were put on women, and I felt my destiny was more than to marry, have children, and keep a home. There were many more opportunities open to men, and I intended to seize some.

Life was already different as I galloped into town and brought it down to a trot. I was so used to being in a dreaded dress that being in men's clothing was freeing. I was looked at differently right away. A few smiles from the ladies boosted my confidence as I came to a halt and hitched my horse at the recruiting station. When I walked through the doors, I knew I passed as a genuine man when the recruiting officer stood from his desk and hurriedly shook my hand. His grip was firm, but being raised only by a man, I gripped his hand just as firmly.

"How do you do? I'm Sergeant Paddock, the recruiting officer here in New Albany. And you?"

"Sir, I'm Melvin Angus Coffield from Borden," I responded, keeping my voice at a low tone, trying to sound as manly as I could without seeming forced.

"You're awfully young, boy. You've not one whisker on your face," he said as he looked me up and down. "Just how old are you, lad?"

"Eighteen, sir." I lied about my age, making myself two years younger than I actually was because I looked so young.

"Do you have permission from your folks to join? Because you don't look older than sixteen."

"Sir, both of my parents are dead."

"I'm terribly sorry to hear that, young man. Why do you want to join the Army?"

"I want to do more with my life, sir. I figure I can do more good fighting the Rebs than staying home milking cows. I want to stand up for the principles of this country and defend the Union...for good ole' Father Abraham," I offered.

"Well, we're looking for men to fill several regiments. However, my regiment is the Ninety-third Indiana Infantry. You have a rifle, son?"

"Yes, sir. An Enfield musket. I've got a horse, too, if you think he could be of service."

"We can use all the supplies and horses we can get our hands on. Can you pass a physical?"

I knew I could, but I was afraid of being detected. I had no choice but to try, so I answered, "Yes, sir."

"Well then, let's get to it." He directed me toward a back room. When we got there, an old man of about sixty years with gray hair and side whiskers was inside waiting to examine the next enlistee. Sergeant Paddock nudged me forward and into the room. "This is Doc Miller. He'll examine you and tell me if you're fit for service." He closed the door and took his leave.

I stood before the doctor, and before he could even say anything to me, my palms became sweaty and my heart raced, beating hard against my chest. I was scared he would feel my bosom and find the cloth bandages that pressed my breasts close to my body. But all he did was simply take his index finger and tap it on my chest a couple of times. He then asked me to open my mouth, and he looked at my teeth. "You in good health, boy?" he asked.

"Why yes, sir."

He guided me back to the door I came through, and when I was outside, he peeked his head around, and yelled, "He's fit."

I walked back to the sergeant, where he sized me up with his eyes and handed me a uniform he thought would fit. "Go try it on. In there." He pointed to a dressing room off to the side. I went in and made sure the door was locked before undressing and replacing my shirt with a white blouse that I buttoned up. Then I pulled up the light blue trousers. I put on the brogans he had given me as well and tied them good. Once that was done, I put on the navy wool coat, and finished the look with a dark blue forage cap. The uniform was a bit big and loose on me, but I knew I could alter it. I looked in the mirror and could not believe my eyes. I was a soldier.

The last thing he did before sending me to camp was have me make my mark on the enlistment papers. I signed up for three years, and would make a salary of thirteen dollars a month. When I looked at the stack of enlistment papers for others, I noticed some were signed with only an X. My father had taught me well, and I knew how to sign my name. However, I had only ever signed my name Melody Ann Coffield. I had to be careful not to make a mistake as I scrolled these papers. He handed me a pen, I dabbed it in the inkwell, and consciously signed Melvin Angus Coffield on the line provided. I was now a private in the 93rd Indiana Infantry of the United States Army, and I could not have been prouder.

Sergeant Paddock led me around the corner and into a fenced-in expanse. Once inside, small white pup tents were lined up by what seemed the hundreds. It was a tent city, and where I would spend the next two months before leaving Indiana. He led me down the row to a tent that stood near a big hickory tree, and I was glad when I was told to stop right in front of it. The temperatures were still high and the sun was blazing, so the shade from this old hickory tree was a welcome one. "This will be your new home until we board for Tennessee," he said, then pointed toward a brick structure about fifty yards away. "Go over to the Quartermaster and get the rest of the gear you'll need. Your immediate superior, and leader of your company, is Captain Woodrow." He must have seen the concern on my face, being a new recruit and all, because he gave me a healthy wallop to my back. It sent me forward and off-balance for a moment. "Don't worry, son. We'll make a soldier out of you yet. Now settle in."

He expected no response as he turned and walked away through a throng of tents and men, and disappeared. When I peered inside the tent, I saw a soldier lying on his back with his eyes closed, his arm draped across his forehead. I knelt to the ground and crawled in, which startled him to attention. "Oh, hello," he said, and quickly sat up. I recognized him right away. Unfortunately, he recognized me as well. I was unmasked. "Melody," he yelled out.

"Teddy, hush," I whispered loudly, placing my index finger over my lips to quiet him.

"What in God's name do you think you're doing?" he asked, stunned and wide-eyed.

"Teddy, I need you to be quiet for just a moment so I can explain."

Theodore Baker was a fellow Borden resident. His family owned a cornfield that spread over many acres of land. He had actually shown an interest in me when we were about the age of thirteen, but neither of his parents approved of their son courting a girl like me. They had no idea that I wanted nothing to do with Teddy that way. I knew my own self, even at thirteen. He and his father used to come to the farm for milk quite often, but for whatever reason that had tapered off after some time.

"My father died," I said, not sure how else to begin.

"Oh dear. I am sorry, Melody."

"Not Melody, Ted. Melvin."

"I don't understand." He was baffled beyond words.

"I couldn't take the melancholy of losing my father, and not having him to help me with the farm just made me realize that I want more. I want to see the country, different places. I want to fight for our nation's cause, and I can't do either of these things while being a woman."

"So, you became a man?"

I nodded.

"Jesus, Melody."

"Teddy, you don't use such language. Stop that. And stop calling me Melody."

"You cannot be a soldier," he said, and leaned forward toward me. "You are not a man. You're a woman disguising yourself as a man, and I won't have it." He began to get up as if to go tell someone, and I grabbed his forearm. He turned to look at me.

"Please, Ted. I'm begging you. Please don't make me go back to the lonely existence my life has become. I don't want to live like that anymore. Please." I beseeched him, pleading my case.

"I don't know, Melo…" He stuttered over my name, and my eyes locked with his. I tried to silently convey all the desperate and righteous parts of me that could not, would not, go back to the misery of my pathetic life. His face softened, and he seemed to receive my message before he spoke. "All right, Melvin. Come on. I'll take you to the Quartermaster to get the things you'll need to be a real and complete Union soldier." He smiled at me, and I at him. I extended my hand like a man would to shake his, and he obliged.

I walked next to him as he led the way. We passed

by tent after tent. Some men were lounging in front of their shelters, playing cards and smoking cigars. Other men formed a circle and let loose a pair of cocks that attacked each other at once. Wagers were placed on one or the other. As we passed the group, the amount of cursing and swearing I heard was almost too much for my own ears to take. I turned back one more time when we were beyond them, and saw feathers flying haphazardly through the air. I couldn't tell which bird was winning, but someone was about to win a lot of loot and a lovely fowl supper.

The Quartermaster's building wasn't much to look at, as it was built with brown bricks. Once inside the room, my eyes had to adjust to the dim ambiance. Not much light entered through the one square window in the front. We walked up to the counter, and the officer behind greeted us without much gusto. "What do you need?"

Without hesitation, Teddy rattled off the items that were essential. "A haversack, a cartridge belt and sling, cap box, ammunition, bayonet and scabbard." I looked at him, having no idea of his quick knowledge of such things. "I haven't been a soldier very long, but there are a few things I picked up on right away," he admitted, then looked to the officer behind the counter once more. "A blanket, plate and cup, fork and spoon."

The officer went to gathering the items he requested, then dumped them all on the counter. No more words were spoken as he went back to puffing on his cigar. I scooped up my new belongings, and before we even made it out the door, he pulled out a small flask and took a swig. My eyes connected with his, and he nodded his disapproval of what he clearly thought was judgement on my part. "Go on now, youngin'," he said sharply, hastening me out the door.

"Come on, Mel," Teddy said, grabbing me by the shoulder and nudging me along in the direction of our tent. When we got back, he told me to put my gear in the tent and come back out. He wanted to take me around while he had a chance. It wouldn't be much longer until our company, Company B, was filled to capacity with newly enlisted soldiers. Until then, we waited. And while we waited, we watched. He took me to an open field where they had dress parades and drills. The 81st Indiana Infantry was on the field now.

We looked on as the troops were drawn up in line, and the order "Parade rest!" was given by each captain to his command. The band beat off and marched down and back in front of the regiment. The officers took four steps to the front, the major and lieutenant colonel in advance of the rest. Teddy pointed out the sergeant's march to the center of the column where he made his report to the adjutant. The adjutant then reported to the colonel and stepped behind him. Then there was a brisk exercise in arms, and the order of "Parade rest!" was repeated. The officers sheathed their swords, proceeded to the center, faced the colonel, and under the lead of the adjutant, marched up to him. They touched their hats as they approached and encircled him to hear his remarks and orders, after which the regiment broke up into companies, and each marched to its quarters under the lead of their sergeants.

It was a striking spectacle to behold, and one of which I would soon be a part. It was frightening, this not knowing, and yet exceedingly exciting. When nighttime fell and "Taps" was played by the bugler, all lights were expected to be out, all noises were to cease, and every enlisted man must be inside his quarters. Teddy lay on his side, having taken off just his uniform jacket. He chose to sleep in his trousers and blouse. "You don't have to be so uncomfortable staying in your uniform. That's no way to sleep. I promise there's nothing you have that I want to see," I said, giving him the freedom to undress further. He giggled a bit, and I finally asked, "What is it? What's so funny?"

"I'm not stripping down to my skivvies because reveille comes early around here, and they expect us out and in line in full uniform for roll call. A lot of the men sleep in their uniforms so they don't have to fall over themselves getting dressed. They don't give us much time to get in line. And that damn bugle just keeps trumpeting away until all are up and trying to rid sleep from their eyes." He rose up on his elbow and squinted his eyes at me. "I suggest you do the same, especially in your condition."

"My condition?" I asked somewhat snidely, knowing what he was going to say next.

"You're a woman. Seriously, Mel, do you really think you're going to be able to step up and be a real soldier? Like a man?"

"I resent your words, Ted. You don't know me. You haven't known me since we were thirteen, and you have no idea how I've been tested by God. This is another test. Without my father, I have no one." I thought for an instant about Violet. Her beautiful face so clearly shone in my mind. My heart froze in time, and though I couldn't mention her to him, I just continued. "I have nothing else to live for. I've decided to live for the Army and Father Abe. I will be a soldier, and I'll be it just as good as a man. I'll prove it to you."

He snickered under his breath again, and simply said, "Goodnight, Private."

I rolled my blanket up and placed it under my head. "Goodnight, Private," I replied. I lay there for an eternity, sleep coming restlessly to me. Thoughts and images of Violet kept returning. Our nights of passion reenacted in my head as I lay there yearning for her, so empty inside without her presence in my life. My heart knew no other love but hers, and this separation that had plagued us was forever. That was the part I couldn't get past. That was the part I couldn't get over. I ached for her love. But she was to marry, and with marriage came children. The next time I saw her, if ever again, she would more than likely have several offspring. I cursed the thought. Eventually, sleep forced itself upon me, and just as Ted had said, reveille came quickly.

❧ ❧ ❧ ❧

The bugler blasted his horn with such force and stamina that attention was involuntary. Getting up was not optional. The sound of men fumbling over one another in the still fairly dark sky was just as loud as the horn. But that horn! That incessant horn, with its blast of sharp, quick notes, could be heard throughout the town. My God, the lungs on that boy.

Ted crawled out of the tent first. "Hurry, or he'll give you extra duty," he yelled. I scampered out behind him, practically running to get in line with the other men. I looked around as others scurried and tripped over their own underdrawers, attempting to line up. While still organizing our line, First Sergeant Upton came to the center and began calling the roll. He didn't require that the men turn out with arms, but he expected us all to stand at attention.

The one thing I learned immediately was that everything we did throughout the day was signaled by one of a number of bugle calls, twenty-six in all. When the morning call was over, we were allowed back to our dwellings to finish with the toilet or even get a few more minutes of shut-eye while the sergeant made his daily report. About thirty minutes after the first call of the day was the breakfast call, or what I came to know as *peas on a trencher.*

We grabbed our plates and cups, and stood in line for a piece of meat, a potato, a chunk of bread, and a cup of coffee with a spoonful of brown sugar in it. There was no milk or butter, unless a soldier wanted to pay for it, so we tended to go without. We settled down into small groups, and soon the meal was over. When I looked over at Ted, he had wiped his plate clean with the rest of his bread, and nearly ate the dish rag. "Hungry?" I asked.

He grunted in between chewing, which he did with his mouth gaping open, and said, "You eat when you can, or you don't eat. Understand that at once."

Even though I wasn't hungry further, I was inclined to finish what was on my plate after hearing him say that. Shortly after breakfast was sick call for the ailing, and fatigue call for the well. The sick were lined up and marched down to the regimental surgeon for examination and prescription. Fatigue duty consisted of policing the company grounds and tidying up the quarters, digging drainage ditches, cutting wood, and similar activities.

If not on a detail, the rest of us were to drill. And drill again. And then, drill some more. Because we were a new unit, our drill consisted mainly of exercises in the handling of arms, practicing various positions and facings, and performing the simple maneuvers of a squad. It taught us to stand erect, face left or right, salute, march forward, to the rear, by the flank, and obliquely. It was a lot to take in and absorb. I fumbled around at first, stepping out of pace with the rest of the men. I wasn't the only one, though. I noticed others that couldn't seem to find their feet about them, and that made me feel a bit better about things. But the fact that they drilled, drilled, drilled, meant that I had time to practice, and before I knew it, marching became second nature, as did the orders and calls. "About face!" I stood at attention. "Forward march!" I stepped off with my right foot and kept pace.

I learned how to load my rifle promptly, but could only get off two shots in one minute. To be an expert shot, I had to pull off three. Although the Army did not require a soldier to get off all three shots in a minute, it did mean you were a good soldier if you could. And I was hellbent on being a good soldier. I wanted—no, I needed—to be a good soldier. It was necessary for me to prove that I could not only do what a man did, but do it better than him. Beyond that, the better soldier I became, the more I might gain the respect of the other men. I hoped that the more respect I had from other soldiers and my superiors, the less scrutiny they would pay me.

I didn't have a struggle with the parry and thrust of the bayonet; that came quite naturally. However, achieving that three-shot goal drove me to the brink of madness. Day in and day out, drill after drill, I strived to get that third shot off. Nerves of steel were required as an officer stood right next to me, his face merely an inch away from mine while he screamed at the top of his lungs. "Do it! Load! Now! Do it now! What's wrong with you, soldier? Faster! Faster!" The veins on his head protruded from his skin. The blood rushed to his face. His voice echoed louder and louder as spit sprayed from his mouth to my cheek. He was looking to distract me in any way possible, all while I tried to load and get a shot off quickly. Anything else was unacceptable and subpar.

We had drilled and practiced for a month when the order to load was given once more. I retrieved a cartridge from my cartridge box, ripped the paper cartridge with my teeth, and poured the powder and the ball down the muzzle. I then rammed the ball and powder to the breech of the barrel, replaced the ramrod, and primed the weapon with a percussion cap. Quickly I cocked and aimed my rifle, and fired. "Again," it was ordered. When I finally got that third shot off, I immediately went to the head of the class. My officers started to recognize my grit and will to fight, and my efforts slowly started to pay off. As I started to load my weapon once more, tearing the cartridge with my teeth fiercely, I realized I was not only an enlisted soldier, but a well-trained soldier. And the soldier life suited me. I was good at it. It was something I could live for.

Chapter Seven

Sunday afternoon was free time for the men. I sat in front of our tent and spit on the buttons of my uniform jacket, shining them with a rag. I enjoyed the mid-fall sun, sitting only in my white uniform blouse. I had yet to strip all the way down. I took off only one item at a time inside our tent, to taper and alter my uniform so it fit better, until it was finally finished. It fit me properly now, and I was to take care of it and any other property given me by the United States Government.

Ted was across from me, cleaning his weapon. He had been brooding over the attention being shown me by the officers of our company.

"Ted, please speak to me," I said as I took my kepi off and set it down. "I can't stand your silence any longer. It's driving me mad."

"You're a girl." He pointed out what we both already knew.

"All right," I replied.

"You're not supposed to be good at this kind of work. Military work," he said. His eyes scanned the men walking past, then back at me as he continued. "How could it be that you are better at it than me?" He put his head down and shook it back and forth, obviously feeling disgraced as a man. Ted hadn't been the soldier he thought he was. He thought that by being born a man naturally, he would find this life easier than a female would.

He started to fidget, and then he became indignant. "I'm going to tell them about you."

"Don't be a rat, Ted. It's not my fault that I'm better at certain things than you."

"What kind of a woman disguises herself as a man? Are you some kind of freak? A pervert? Maybe a whore?"

I slapped him straight across his cheek. "How dare you? I may be a girl, but I'll whip you yet."

"Them's fighting words for such a pretty young lad. You sure you want me to humiliate you in front of your comrades? Maybe I'll show them what's really under that uniform. Would you like that?" His eyes pierced through me. He didn't take kindly to being threatened by someone of the female persuasion. Especially one that could shoot off three accurate rounds in one minute to the one he could barely get off while the sergeant yelled in his face. I never let that sergeant get to me. I went somewhere else when he barked his orders and pleaded that my pace be quickened. It was as if it was just me and the rifle. I tuned it out. Ted couldn't.

Essentially, I knew he could very well do what he had threatened and expose me. He growled. "You know, when the sergeant yelled at me and asked me why I couldn't be as good a soldier as Private Coffield, I should have spoken up about you then."

He got up and started toward the officers' quarters. "Ted, wait." I followed, tugged on his shoulder, and added, "I beg of you."

"Why did you have to join the Army? Why couldn't you stay home and marry a man and have children like the rest of the girls?"

"Ted, I've already answered you as best I can. I really don't know. Honestly, I don't think I knew who I was until I came here. I feel like I've found my calling. Like I'm supposed to be here, for a long duration or short. Only God knows." I lowered my head in anticipated defeat. "I don't know how long I'll be able to keep up this farce. Let's face it, at any time I could be found out. Please don't be the one to send me back to my miserable existence in Borden."

Just then, an officer happened by. I looked to Ted, my eyes pleading with him to keep my secret. "Please?" I reiterated.

He pierced his lips together in disgust and shook his head slightly back and forth. "You owe me," he snapped, and added, "Stop making me look so bad."

After that day, it was all I could do to keep Ted happy. I didn't stop trying to be the best soldier I could be. No, I could not lessen myself to that. It was bad enough belonging to the weaker sex. I would not allow that weakness to seep into me now that I was successfully presenting as a man. I couldn't help it if Ted wasn't the most skilled or talented soldier. He lacked the discipline it took, and I was schooled properly by my father on the subject.

⁂

One day, when we were on some free time, he was spit shining his brogans. I noticed his stockings had several holes and tears in them. "You know, Ted, I could mend those socks for you." My offer was an effort to keep myself in his good graces.

"You sew?" he asked, almost surprised.

"I do, and I'm damned good at it." I immediately

regretted my choice of words, remembering how he felt about me being better than him at soldiering. I thought maybe I should tone my confidence down in this instance.

A suggestion of annoyance hovered in his eyes, but then dissipated into sudden gratitude. "I would appreciate it."

"Hand 'em over."

He pulled them from his feet and gave them to me. I pulled my small sew kit out of my haversack and poked the thread through the hole of the needle. I stitched and repaired what I could as he watched me intently.

"Some of the boys are getting together after supper tonight. Private Wells plays the banjo and the boys get to singing. Would you like to join us?"

I was a bit taken aback, since he had just recently threatened to turn me in to our higher-ranking officers. However, I accepted his invitation, wanting to fit in with the rest of the men.

After a subpar supper of boiled beef and beans, Ted and I walked over to Private Wells's tent, a couple of tent streets over from us. As we approached, we could already hear the melodious voices of a small group of soldiers huddled around a campfire. Private Wells picked at the strings of his instrument, and every now and again would chime in with his own voice.

We sat with the rest around the fire and began singing "The Battle Cry of Freedom." Ted and I looked at each other, and for the first time I felt included and a part of something truly amazing. "Yes, we'll rally around the flag boys, we'll rally once again, shouting the battle cry of freedom! The Union forever! Hurrah, boys, hurrah!" We sang in unison, a sense of patriotic pride taking over as we bellowed out the words. With arms over the shoulders of the men sitting next to us, we all swayed and sang. It wasn't until the final call of the night, and the bugler sounding his horn with "Taps," that we finally called it a night and dispersed in the direction of our quarters.

It was that night that Ted and I finally became friends. And with each passing day, drilling, learning, and parading, my company became a force to be reckoned with, or so we thought. We had never been tested in the thick of real battle. The discipline of drilling was satisfying to me. Guard duty was not. Boring would make it sound too exciting. Tedious, mind-numbing silence was all to be had standing guard. Most of my time at this duty was spent trying not to fall asleep while standing up. Nighttime guard duty was the worst—just me, the stars, and more silence. Nothing to do, being left alone with only my thoughts. Thoughts that still drifted back to Violet and the weight of my still broken heart. Soldiering was the only thing that filled the void there.

❧❧❧❧

September and October passed like a flash. Before I knew it, November was upon us and our marching orders were given. Our superior officers informed us we would be boarding a train for Memphis, Tennessee on November 9. When that date arrived, company by company, we marched to the train depot. The lead locomotive was elaborately decorated with banners, and a handmade sign posted to the very front that read, *Death to Traitors.*

The conditions inside of the train were horrendous as soldiers were stuffed into the confines. Boxcars were equipped with backless benches of rough plank, and inadequately, if at all, provided with heat, ventilation, food, water, and sanitary facilities. Men hurrahed and imbibed as they hung out the windows waving to the girls and asking for kisses.

Women and children alike came to see us off. They held patriotic flags and signs, and cheered for our anticipated victories. We were making our home state of Indiana proud of her sons. Us Hoosiers intended to fight with honor and dignity. The Army band played as we all sang the favorite going away song for the war, the soul-stirring "John Brown's Body."

The whistle blew and the train slowly began chugging down the track. A plume of steam escaped the engines, leaving a long trail of smoke above the moving locomotive. Inferior tracks and poor roadbeds made for a rough and bumpy ride. Several breakdowns and two days later, we arrived in Memphis hungry and exhausted.

❧ ❧ ❧ ❧

Fort Pickering was a defense occupied by the Confederates until June 6, 1862, when Union gunboats arrived on the Mississippi River and a naval battle ensued. The battle for Memphis lasted an hour and a half, and when it was all said and done, all but one Confederate boat was destroyed. The remaining Rebel troops retreated farther south. With newly recruited colored troops, the Union Army enlarged and expanded several areas of the fort, stretching it two miles along the South Memphis bluffs. It was outfitted with fifty-five guns, and included structures needed to serve the large number of troops living in Memphis and those passing through. Buildings in the fort included a hospital, rail depot, water works, and sawmill.

It was cleaner, more organized, and way bigger than the camp we came from in New Albany. We settled in quickly. The funny thing about the state of Tennessee was that the eastern part remained heavily pro-union, while the western part of the state was all for secession. They were split down the center on whether they believed in either cause.

Winter was soon approaching, and I was thankful we didn't have to sleep in tents. Our quarters were a bit crammed and damp. However, having a fortified shelter from the wind and elements was received with great appreciation. There were some tents, mostly Sibleys, but they appeared to be used by troops just passing through.

Once inside our shelter, there was a big room filled with bunk-style beds. The other barracks were the same. This one was large enough to fit our entire company of Hoosiers, fifty in all. We spread out, choosing our beds, and I promptly chose a top bunk. We would be here for a stay, and I picked a bed close to the potbelly stove, rather than over by the window which so many fought over.

I must say, I was surprised to see Ted choose the lower bunk below mine. He put his pack down on the mattress and peered up at me. His slight smile was all I needed to tell me he finally thought of me as a friend and ally, not a feeble, delicate woman. A soldier. I didn't think he would ever think of me as a true man. Perhaps he wouldn't, but he made it clear through his facial expression that he did think of me as a soldier.

I smiled back at him, and he said, "We've got some free time tonight. A bunch of the boys are going into the city. Would you like to join us?"

My heart was elated, as I was slowly being accepted into the ranks. "Sure. I would like that."

⚜ ⚜ ⚜ ⚜

When evening came about, twelve of us in all took the short walk into town. It was Saturday night, and the saloons were packed with men seeking to quench their thirst with a little snort. Beale Street was lined with saloons and brothels. I was shocked by the multitude, since Borden had only one saloon and no brothels. And really, they might have just as well gotten rid of the sole saloon and replaced it with a church. Churches—now there was something Borden had plenty of. Liquor was Satan's elixir.

The boys were thrilled to be out of camp and doing something fun. The break in the mundaneness of soldier life was a welcome one. While we walked down the street, Ted offered me a pinch of tobacco. He had some stuffed inside his cheek, and every now and again he would spit a hunk out. I took a bit, but my confusion and lack of experience warranted him to instruct me. "That pinch you have between your fingers, put that between your lips and gum. Wait until the juice builds up in your mouth and then spit the juice out. Like this." He swished the tobacco around in his cheek and spit the liquid out. "Now you."

I stuck it inside my lip. It burned. The taste was more than gross. Strands of the leafy tobacco migrated all over my mouth, and rather than spit, it seemed a long line of drool escaped as I gagged and did all I could not to vomit. He struck me on the back a few times and said, "If you want to be a man, Mel, you'll have to do things that men do. Try again. Scoop it all up with your tongue and push it back behind your lip. Go on."

I did as he said, but my face wouldn't stay straight. I looked as though I had eaten a mouthful of lemons with my eyes squinted and lips pursed. The gross taste of the tobacco was enough to turn me green, but I wanted to fit in. I tried again. My tongue would never forgive me as it corralled the tobacco together and pushed it between my lip and gum. Finally able to keep a straight face, I insisted that my mouth adapt and adjust to the taste and texture. Juice filled in the pocket of my cheek and I was forced to spit or swallow, and as the latter was not an option my stomach could handle, I spit. A tiny dribble dripped out of the corner of my mouth as I did. With a little more practice, I was able to get the hang of it. "That a gir—" He caught himself before he finished his sentence. My eyes were wide as he gathered his thoughts and refrained. "That a boy, Mel!" He patted my back in approval.

The rest of the group walked in front of us and were too busy talking to one another to even care what we were discussing. All but one: Corporal Albert Turner. When Ted made his faux pas by almost referring to me as a girl, Albert's head whipped around to spy on us. His forehead wrinkled in the center of his brows and his eyes bore into me. "How old did you say you were, Coffield?" he asked suddenly.

"Nineteen," I answered. "Why?"

"You ain't never learned to chew tobaccie? Didn't your pappy ever teach you?"

"My father smoked cigars, so no, he never taught

me." I thought I was in the clear with my quick reply.

But he pressed on. "You ever drink whiskey?"

"I haven't."

"Ever been with a lady?"

"Excuse me?"

"Come on now, Coffield. Spill it. Have you ever given a girl a green gown?"

I knew he was referring to sex, and my nerves had gotten the best of me. I was uncomfortable with his line of questioning, and Ted knew it. "Leave him alone, Turner. It's none of your damned business." I knew Ted was trying to protect me, but I answered anyway.

"Actually, no I haven't. And I'm more of a gentleman than giving a girl a green gown."

"Gentleman? What are you? Some kind of sissy boy?"

Ted took hold of Albert's arm and spun him around. Then, he grabbed hold of his uniform jacket and cocked his fist back ready to punch Albert square in the face. "I swear to the Devil himself, if you don't shut your bone box, you'll be getting a nice black blinker from me."

"Why do you keep defending this bully trap? Are you going on with him?" Albert egged him on.

The other men, who had gotten a few steps ahead of us, stopped dead in their tracks as they heard the ruckus behind them. This was not at all how this outing was supposed to go. I ventured out tonight to see the city and get to know some of the other men I would be fighting beside, not to see them fight with each other.

I couldn't have the others suspecting not only me, but Ted too, of any funny business. I gathered my courage and stepped up to the two men clutching one another's breast. I pushed Ted to the side, and with all the power I could muster, hauled off and punched Albert across the nose. He was slightly taller than me, and being a natural-born man meant he possessed natural-born strength. I used my fear of a severe ass-kicking, and the fear of being found out, to attack him again, dodging forward and leading with my fist. I socked his nose once more, and he fell backward and onto the ground.

He lay there on his back for a moment before sitting up, holding his nose in his hands as blood rushed out, down his face, and through his fingers, dripping onto his uniform jacket. "You broke my nose!" He yelled in pain.

I chose to finish as a true gentleman would, and offered him my hand to help him up. He looked at me with pure disgust in his eyes, but he took my hand anyway. I pulled him back to his feet, and although he didn't speak to me right away, I knew I had earned his respect.

The other men looked to me, and then at each other, and burst into incredible laughter at the sight they had just witnessed. They hooted and hollered, and shuffled me into the saloon of their choosing. Kicking open the double swinging doors, they led me straight to the bar. One of my comrades, Private Bradley Huntley, caught my attention, and said, "We're going to swill tonight, young man."

"But I've never had a swig."

He laughed a hearty laugh from the pit of his belly and forewarned me, "You're about to sluice your gob, my little friend." He was more than excitable when he turned to the barkeeper. "Give me a bottle of your cheapest rye."

In turn, the barkeeper set a bottle down and six shot glasses. He filled them with the golden liquid, and all of us dug through our pockets to help pay for it. One by one, we picked up our glasses. "Into the sauce box it goes." Bradley saluted and raised his glass.

I had never tasted spirits before, and I truly didn't know what to expect. I knew if it were anything like tobacco, it would be ghastly. "Come now, Mel. Don't be poked up. Drink!"

I wanted to assimilate to male behaviors and have a place with my peers, so with the rim of the glass on my lips, I tilted my head back and opened up my mouth, letting the whiskey go down freely and quickly. Not expecting it to set fire to my throat, blazing a trail to my stomach and landing like a bomb, my belly rejected it, and it came right back up, spraying the bartender standing directly in front of me.

The boys laughed boisterously, all finding it hysterically funny. All but the bartender, who had already looked like he was a Southern sympathizer, along with a bunch of other miserable-looking characters in the place. I could tell he didn't take kindly to serving booze to Yankees, and even less kindly to being spit on by one. He wiped his face with a towel, looked at me, and said, "No more of that. Ya understand?"

Corporal Andrew L. Greene, a burly, broadbacked man, simply drew open his uniform jacket, flashed his pistol at the bartender, and ordered, "Pour him another and keep your mouth shut." He then turned to me. "Keep this one down."

Six more shots were filled. Again, Bradley saluted and toasted. "Cheers to the boys in blue." We all clinked glasses and chugged the whiskey down. I had a better idea of what to expect, and I quickly drank it. My face squished up, still not liking the taste at all, but I kept it down this time. We all placed our glasses on the bar and finally took a moment to survey our surroundings.

Tables were filled with men drinking and gambling as a musician played the piano in the corner of the room by a stage, where women dressed in low-cut fitted dresses with a slit all the way up both sides danced to the music in harmony. The intricate, fancy headdresses they wore included an array of red and green feathers that matched the green of their dresses.

In the center of the floor was a dance area where the girls would dance with the men. Sounds of loud talking, and bottles and glasses being clinked together filled the room, which also filled with tobacco smoke and the stench of stale beer. "Why don't you ask one of these scarlet ladies for a dance?" Bradley asked.

"Oh, I don't know. I don't think so."

"Why not? Got a sweetheart back home?"

"No, nothing like that," I said.

"Well, come on. We'll both go ask for a dance then." He paused for a moment in thought, and added, "But not before one more shot."

Chapter Eight

Bradley grabbed the bottle and poured out the shot. Granted, I had spit out my first one. The second had sizzled its way down and stayed put. That one had barely had time to settle in as I took the glass he handed me.

"Cheers to indulging in a bit of fruitful vine tonight." He chugged the golden elixir and waited for me to do the same. I didn't care for his rude way of speaking of ladies, but men were less refined than their more sensitive counterparts, and in this environment it was acceptable. It had to be. I bit my tongue from chastising his use of euphemisms and snapped my head back as I dumped the fiery liquid down my anticipating throat.

Without speaking, he lightly put his hand on my shoulder and directed me through the crowd of people. We approached a group of ladies huddled together by the pianist, and the smiles and girly giggles that came from them were welcoming and friendly.

"Well, hello there, Billy Yanks." A lovely girl with long brunette hair greeted us.

"Care to dance, darlin'?" Bradley asked, getting right to it.

She didn't bother to answer. Rather, she took his hand and led him to the dance floor. Before he was out of reach, he shoved me forward and into one of the lovely maidens. Not wanting to disappoint my jovial comrade, I tipped my hat to the young girl and apologized. "Sorry, miss. My friend is somewhat impaired and completely obnoxious."

Her cheeks blushed a bright red against the fairness of her freckled skin, and in the sweetness of her voice, asked, "Would you like to dance with me?"

She extinguished my stress of having to ask her, and I politely accepted. "Indeed. Yes, I would be honored."

She led the way to the dance floor, and as a slow melody began to play, she gently placed one hand on my shoulder while the other was placed in mine. Dancing wasn't my forte. The few times my father had joked with me, twirling me around the room, were fun and happy times. But they were rare times and I never got the hang of it. Even if I had, I would have been forced to learn the woman's part in it. A man was to lead in the dance. I had no idea how to lead, and trying to explain that was almost impossible as the liquor had now started to take effect.

A lightness of my head pervaded, and the more she smiled, the more I smiled back. It was involuntary, as if my body had a mind of its own. I would soon learn that whiskey took control of the mouth, and voice as well, a vulnerability I could not afford to surrender in my situation.

"I'm not much of a dancer, as you can plainly see," I said while I awkwardly tried to mimic the other couples on the floor. "I'm dancing with this pretty girl, and tripping over two left feet. My apologies."

She lifted my chin with her fingers, as my eyes were glued to our feet. "It's all right. You just need some practice," she said while we swayed back and forth. "My name is Sadie Harper. What's yours?"

"Melvin Coffield," I replied.

"Well, Melvin, how 'bout another drink?"

"I don't know. I think the men are almost ready to go back to camp."

"Are you sure about that?" She pointed to Bradley, who was now climbing the stairs to one of the rooms there, led by the woman he was just dancing with. He glanced down at me and gave a small wink, pointing to me in gesture that I should follow suit. I had no intentions of going anywhere but back to the fort.

Sadie had other plans for me, though. She led me back to the bar and proceeded in the continuation of my inebriation. Had I just stopped at two, I may have gotten back to camp like I intended. However, Sadie insisted on sharing in a swig with me. I noticed the other men I came here with were fired up. A couple were dancing, a couple were still drinking, but another couple appeared to want more than dance and drink, getting a little cocky with the Southern sympathizers in the room.

I couldn't get involved with that currently, though, as Sadie handed me a glass filled with more whiskey. This one went down fairly smooth. In the case of drinking alcohol, I realized the more I drank, the easier it flowed down one's gullet. My head not only became light, but was a bit dizzy as well. After the fifth one, my mouth took on a will of its own and my balance was no longer even. If I didn't know better, I'd swear the room was on a full tilt to the right. Like a magnet, I was pulled to the right every time I took a step. Traipsing back to the dance floor with Sadie seemed a complicated task, but once out there, my confidence grew as I took her in my arms and rocked her to a soft tune.

I wasn't expecting it when she pressed up close to my body. Her head rested on my shoulder, and the sweet smell of wildflowers burst through my senses. The old feelings that I had for women erupted in me once more. All that I had done to stop these perverse thoughts seamlessly dissipated when she placed her head on me.

She was quite lovely, and she appeared to take a shine to me. The thought of her finding out my truth caused me a great deal of anxiety. And although I knew I should say as little as possible, my senses were altered as was my mouth. "You're very beautiful, you know?" I knew I shouldn't compliment her, but I had no say over what came through my very drunken lips.

Her strawberry blond hair was pulled back, with ringlets of curls loosely cascading down her neck. Her eyes were cobalt blue, and the softness in them was evident as she looked at me with adoration. She was a young girl, not as mature as the other women. Her cleavage was exposed from the low-cut dress she wore, and I could not peel my eyes from them. Even while I fought with myself in my head, screaming to avert my stare, she smiled at me, welcoming my attention.

While we exchanged gazes, acknowledging our attraction for each other, we traded stories of our lives. She was from a small town just outside of Memphis. Things were tense at home, and with her being one of the oldest children in a line of many offspring, her parents forced her out of their house. They would have preferred her to get married, but after she was sexually attacked by the man they promised her to, they felt she was tainted for every other man, and made her leave the family home.

She said she left for the city of Memphis, hoping to find work enough to survive on her own. When she arrived, there was no work to be had. A single female with no education and no money was not a useful thing to be, so rather than become hungry and homeless, she wandered into this saloon and boarding house. The working women quickly took her under their wing and taught her how to make fast money. They told her she'd never be hungry again. Of course, she didn't immediately realize that they were speaking of prostitution. Having lost her virginity through rape, it seemed an easy choice. She never did care for it, but after two years of pleasuring men, she became numb to it.

"Men aren't usually so nice to me. Not like you anyway," she said, still swaying to the music. "There's something different about you."

"I don't believe in treating a lady poorly, my dear. Your worth doesn't lie between your legs," I said, acknowledging for the first time tonight that I genuinely liked her. "Your worth lies here." I pointed to her head and, controlled by the rye, took her gaze and beheld it before leaning in to kiss her. She had been wanting me to, even though she never said so. She didn't have to. Her lips received mine invitingly, and the softness, the moistness of them sent warm sensations downward past my abdomen where there should be none.

"Come to my room for a nightcap," she whispered.

"I can't. It's getting late, and the boys and I need to get back before curfew," I said, and then just like a blubbering fool, added, "And I don't have any money."

Her insulted stare told me I had uttered the wrong thing. She snapped at me. "Have I asked for any?"

"Sadie, I'm sorry. I didn't mean to be so crass. I just thought—"

Her lips met mine again, quieting my mouth from saying anything more foolish. She wrapped her arms around my neck, and in my ear softly said, "Come back to my room."

"But..." I stuttered, surveying the room for Teddy and any help he could give me in tearing myself away from this lovely yet mysterious young woman.

She turned my panicked face toward her with her fingertips and cut me off. "No buts." I felt her reach for my hand, and I followed as she turned and exclaimed, "Come with me."

With a small tug of my hand, she wound me through the crowd to the same staircase Bradley had, earlier that evening, ascended himself with an adventuress. As I took the first step up, I once again searched the crowd for Ted. And there he was, making not only eye contact with me, but making intense, alarmed eye contact with me. He knew as well as I did that if this girl found me out, I was in deep pig soil. He tried his best to make his way through the throng of people dancing to the stairs. He made it there in just enough time to grab me by the arm and stop my forward motion. Sadie snapped to a halt when I did, and Ted asked, "Where are you going, good chum? It's almost time to go back to camp. We can't be late."

"That's true," I said loudly over the music and conversation of the room, and pointedly loud enough for Sadie to hear and understand. However, there was no understanding. She didn't comprehend—nor did she seem to care to comprehend—the strict rules of the Army.

"You'll be back in plenty of time. You're just coming up for a snort." She looked past me to Ted and told him, "You can wait down here. He won't be long."

She pulled at me once again, and Ted disappeared from my view as we rounded the corner to her boudoir. If I had to be honest with myself, I wanted to be with her in a physical way, but she thought I was a man. Her frightened reaction was anticipated, and being cornered like a threatened animal was an uncomfortable feeling.

Once inside the confines of her bedroom, she lit the gas lantern. While she did, I took a look around. The flame from the candle illuminated the room enough that I could see her bed up against the center of the wall. A homespun quilt lay across it. A meager dresser and a small desk were the only furniture in the tiny room.

From her desk, she pulled a metal flask and two tumblers. She filled them both and handed me one. I was already pigeon-eyed and out of my wits, and my lesson would be learned after taking it from her. She raised her glass. "To love, loyalty, and length of days." We clinked and swallowed, and what had once burned going down now drank as if it were water.

The glass was taken from my hand, and I watched her place both glasses down before moving closer to me. Her gaze set on my barely open eyes. My incapacities and vulnerability were easily taken advantage of as she leaned into me, taking her own initiative in kissing my lips. My intoxicated mind battled within itself, my desire versus my secret. The winner became clear as I lost my struggle to her want of me. The gentleness of her lips blazed a trail of passion to my groin, and I pressed her back into the wall, ravaging her mouth and tongue like a beast that had been lying in wait to attack.

Images of Violet flashed before me. Scenes of affection and ardor ran by one by one. In the state I was in, Sadie practically became her, and she allowed me to undress her. I was hungry for her body, and her soft skin filled a yearning inside of me as my fingertips brushed over her bare breasts. Her nipples hardened under my touch, and when I placed my mouth around it, my desire heightened. I needed to feel her now. Her nakedness aroused me to the point of separating her legs with my knee and placing my hand in her pulsating center, which elicited a sharp gasp.

"I didn't know you had it in you, Yankee boy," she said between moans.

"Oh, Violet," I murmured into her ear while we were cheek to cheek. My body had found its way between her thighs, along with my hand, and I ground my hips against her, forcing myself deeper inside of her. Her back slid up and down the wall with every thrust, and without warning, she climaxed. "Ohh… uh-huh! Uh-huh! Yesss! Yesss!" Her arms tightened around my neck, squeezing out the last of her offering, her body shuddering, finally releasing me.

She took my face in her hands and kissed me tenderly. I looked in her eyes and saw my beautiful Violet once more before my mouth filled with vomit, and I shot the cat, not only upon her, but anything close to her. The room spun involuntarily, and all I remember was saying, "I'm sorry" before the lights went out in my head. I fell to the floor in a heap, unconscious, and susceptible to examination.

Chapter Nine

Even though the morning sun shone through the window, the temperature in the room was brisk. I slowly opened my eyes, fluttering them a few times before waking for the day. My head felt like a ton of bricks, groggy and foggy as I tried to lift it, curious as to where I was and what day it happened to be.

"You've got some explaining to do, don't you, Melvin?" I heard from the corner of the room. Sadie stoked a small fire in the fireplace, trying to warm the little space. The wind from outside howled and shook the delicate windows of her bedchamber.

I sat up, and quickly realized my uniform blouse was unbuttoned and laid open. The strap beneath had been hankered with and loosened, barely covering my breasts. My pants had been taken off and I was down to my undergarments. Bewilderment was replaced with horror at the realization of being found out.

"Perhaps some scandal water this morning, yes?" She handed me a cup of tea and shot a deadly gaze at me.

"Not much for tea this morning. Where are the rest of my clothes?" I questioned as I scanned the floor for my garments.

She threw my pants at me, and asked once more, "Would you care to explain why, when I began undressing you, I found breasts instead of a man's chest?"

She was eager for my answer, and I stuttered hopelessly. "I, uh…I, uh…Sadie, I can explain, really. See…I…uh…" I let out a swift breath and tried to regain my composure.

"You need to do better than that, soldier. Soldieress? Is there a word for this? Are you some kind of pervert?" She was clearly upset. "I should turn you in to your superior officer, I should."

"No, no. Sadie, please." I jumped from the bed swiftly while I felt a glazed look of despair spread over my face. "Please don't do that. I'll explain if you'll only let me."

Her eyes were fixed on me sternly as her eyebrows raised in amused contempt at the story I told. A story of an unusual childhood on a dairy farm without siblings and raised by a father who would later die before my very eyes. A story of love and heartbreak, and the lonely existence of my solitary life where I wasn't accepted for who I was, limited by the nature of my sex. I pleaded to her, insisting that keeping my secret would be exciting for her. As a man, I could do certain things for her that maybe she, as a woman, wouldn't be allowed or able to do.

"When you thought I was a man, you liked me an awful lot. Does anyone really need to know?" I said matter-of-factly, waiting patiently for her response. My palms were filled with perspiration, and my heart raced in anticipation, hoping against all hope that she would keep my skeleton in the closet.

After a few minutes of contemplation, Sadie stood from her seated position, straightened her skirt, and said, "I will keep your little secret safe, but you will do something for me."

"Yes, anything," I exclaimed in excitement. "What

is it?"

"When the time is right, I'll let you know." She looked me up and down, as I was dressed and back in my uniform. By the time her gaze traveled the length of my body and back to my eyes, her facial expression had changed from one of sheer betrayal to one of flirtatiousness, the same look she had given me last night. "Like I said, there was something different about you from other men. My God, I would never have thought this." She stepped a tad bit closer to me. "The way you touched me last night…it was unlike how any man has ever touched me. Men are only concerned with their own gratification, but you…" She softly touched the collar of my jacket and brushed her fingers over my cheek. "You were all about pleasing me."

"Did I?" I probed, feeling like I wanted to kiss her, yet feeling a queasiness in my stomach.

"Yes. Very much so." Her head tilted slightly to the right, but just as she was about to kiss me, I covered my mouth with my hand. I reached and grabbed for her chamber pot, thankful that it was clean, and wretched the remnants of my stomach contents.

Once I lifted my head from the pot, I blearily held her gaze and apologized for what seemed the hundredth time that morning. "I'm sorry, Violet."

"Violet? Why do you keep calling me that? It's the second time you've referred to me as such."

"She was my—"

Knock-knock-knock.

Three sharp raps on the door prevented my explanation. Without consent, the door was kicked in violently. Sadie jumped back, and I, too, was startled and jolted back a step. "Melvin! We must go at once."

It was Bradley. He was disheveled beyond belief. His hair was askew as was his uniform, which was half on, half off. His forage cap was cockeyed and his breath reeked of leftover alcohol.

"Bradley, what the hell?"

"No time for all that. We missed our curfew last night. We need to go now before they hang us for desertion. The other men left us here, the ratbags. We must go at once, or face serious repercussions."

He took me by my arm and rushed me out the door. As we turned the corner out of her room, I looked back and said, "I will see you again, Sadie. I promise, I'll return."

⁂

Bradley and I walked the distance back to camp, and though we walked as fast as we could, knowing we were in trouble with our superiors, he still managed to ask me, "Well, how was it?"

I peered over at him, the wrinkles between my eyebrows deepening in consternation, and returned his question. "How was what?"

"It was your first time, yes?"

"First time for what?"

"Why, with the ladies, of course. Did you become a full-fledged man last night?"

At that point, I understood what he was getting at, and in my effort to fit in, I replied, "Yes. Yes, I did."

He gave me a healthy pat on my back, sending me forward as I stumbled some, all the while his laughter filling the silent air. "That a boy! Tell me everything."

"I most certainly will not. I've too much respect

for her."

"Respect? You do know that's what she does for a living, right?"

I tried to disguise my annoyance with his blatant contempt for women. "Yes, Bradley, I know what she does for money."

"Don't be so obtuse, Melvin. And don't go falling in love with a woman like that. No good can come from it."

I chose to ignore him. I would see Sadie again. Not for love, but for female companionship. Being around only men for months now was leaving me feeling melancholy. Feelings of ardor were far from my mind as the pain of losing Violet was still a fresh wound to my heart.

The rest of our trek was a quiet one. Sounds of deep breathing were all that were heard as we practically trotted back to the fort. The closer we got, the faster our pace. We had no idea what our punishment would be, but we anticipated some kind of disciplinary action. When we finally arrived, we were taken immediately to the adjutant general, wherein he doled out a rather filthy punishment. Along with three other offenders breaking curfew, we were to fill in a latrine ditch that was full to capacity, then dig a new ditch for the same purpose. The stench alone was punishment enough. Between the foul odor and the leftover taste of liquor, I vomited my way through the task, even if nothing was left to come out. I would curse Bradley for my woes, but I had no one to blame but myself. The only thing that got me through it was the fact that I'd had such a wonderful time the night before. Fitting in with the boys was essential to keeping my secret sealed tightly. I felt that friendships were developing, and my gender identification was coming together as I was educated on how to be a man—from real men.

The height of my night, however, was meeting a pretty girl. Even more intriguing was that she intended to keep my privileged information to herself. No doubt she was more than curious about me, and my objective while the Army was bivouacked currently was to see Sadie again. I hadn't felt the comfort of a woman since Violet, and although Sadie hadn't touched me, I rather enjoyed the intimacy we shared as I delighted her body's desires. I needed the company of a woman. It was a necessity in my life.

⁂

After the wretched duty of punishment, we were allowed back to our barracks. The end of November drew to a close, and December opened with much boredom and doldrum. Guard duty was boring. Drill was boring. We did the best we could to pass the time, mostly by playing games or sports. We held foot races, of which I came out on top against each man who challenged me. It helped with the induction of my false manhood, and it made me more popular with the others. Wrestling was one of their favorite pastimes, and an activity I steered clear of. I was fit for a woman, but naturally speaking I would be no contest for a man.

The winter was long and cold, and we could hardly wait for spring's arrival, as well as the chance to fight. Remaining idle was getting to us, even driving some of us mad to an extent. Repairing and mending the uniforms for the men had become routine for me, and helped to pass some time. However, my time was quickly further occupied when they learned that I could cut hair. On down time, soldiers would line up for a clean cut and shave.

One day, Bradley sat in my chair, and directed, "Melvin, my good boy, take a little off the sides, and remove my whiskers. Leave the mutton chops, though. The ladies love when they tickle their cheeks."

I snickered, lathered his face with soap, took the straight edge, and began shaving him around the chin. "Grab a pass and go into town later?" he asked with a mischievous grin across his countenance.

"I don't know, Bradley. I don't behave properly around you," I said, recalling our debauchery that night at the saloon several weeks before.

"Are you saying I'm a bad influence on you?"

"That is indeed what I'm saying."

"We had fun though, didn't we?" He chuckled, his shoulders bouncing with each giggle.

"Stop laughing, or you'll have me cut you," I shouted with the razor to his cheek, his laughter becoming contagious in my own guffaw.

"Come on, Mel. You know you want to see that girl again, I can see it in your eyes. Let's go."

I finally gave in, knowing he was right. I did want to see that girl. "All right then. Go on, gather up the other chaps." I finished and wiped off the blade.

"No, no. Just you and I," he said. "It'll be more fun without the stress of keeping a big group of us together."

❧❧❧❧

Later that afternoon, the two of us walked to

town. The temperature was frigid, and the frock coats we wore kept us as warm as possible. Bradley's breath was visible as he spoke. "When we get into town, let's stop at the photographer's shop."

"What for?"

"For a picture of us, of course. I'd like to send one home to my family."

I wasn't too keen on having my likeness taken and reproduced, but I gave in, as his excitement was hardly containable. He was from New York City. Born to a lawyer, he was an only child, as his mother miscarried several times after his birth. They didn't want him to join the military, afraid of losing the only seed they produced. However, honor was foremost, and to not go would have caused townspeople to think him a coward. And that, he insisted, was not true. Sending them his picture would be testament that he was still living.

The town was bustling with people strolling to and fro as horses and carriages trotted down the main street. We found a photographer's shop almost right away. We opened the door, and when the bell attached chimed, a bearded older gentleman appeared. No one else was in the place, and the silence was rather unnerving after having just been in the noisy crowd of travelers outside.

He looked at us awkwardly as he examined our uniforms from head to toe. Once his sight trained on the pistol barely visible under Bradley's slightly opened frock coat, he simply asked, "How can I help you fellers?"

"We would like you to take a photograph of us. Two, actually, one for me and one for my friend."

"That's fine. Step right over here," he said, directing us to a wooden chair in front of an empty wall. "Set yourselves up however you please while I get my camera ready."

We walked over the creaky floorboards to the coatrack in the corner of the room and removed our coats. We kept our kepis on and straightened up one another's uniforms. Bradley guided me by the back to the sole chair in front of the bare wall, and I had a seat. He stood to the left of me, then to the right of me. He stood with his pistol in its holster, and then stood with his pistol out. He did this several times before settling on a pose to the left of me, his one hand on my shoulder, the other displaying his pistol.

The photographer aimed his accordion-like camera at us and draped the attached cloth over his head. "You must stay completely still for ninety seconds for the image to take. I'm going to remove the cap for a flash. Ninety seconds. Be steady now," he ordered.

Ninety seconds didn't seem like long, but when you're trying to stay still for that duration, it became forever. In ninety seconds, my nose itched at least a dozen times and nearly drove me crazy, not being allowed to scratch at it. The seconds ticked slowly and agonizingly by, and perspiration formed above my upper lip. Once the time was up and the image was taken, the clock was reset as we posed without movement for the second image.

By the time it was taken, I was sweating profusely as drops of perspiration dripped off my forehead. The old man dislodged the camera from its stand and started for another room. "Where are you going?" Bradley asked.

"To develop the images. I need to be in the dark

to begin the process," he answered, and restarted for the room.

"I'm curious as to how that's done. Do you mind if I tag along?"

While they spoke, I stood up from the chair. When I turned around, I couldn't help but notice a small blot of blood on the seat. It was just a small cushion, off-white in color, something to take the sting away from sitting on the hard wooden chair for long periods of time. But blood now stained it, and my anxiety level grew to extreme heights as I realized I had gotten my female cycle. My eyes widened and my heart beat out of control at the thought of being discovered. And I would no doubt be discovered if they saw that blood.

"Come on, Mel. Let's observe the making of a daguerreotype photograph." Bradley followed the old man. I didn't budge though, and he appeared puzzled as he turned back to me. "Mel?"

"You go ahead, Bradley. I need to step outside for some fresh air." I wiped the sweat from my brow and stood directly in front of the chair trying to hide the appalling stain.

"Are you feeling all right? You're awfully pale." He started toward me.

"I'm fine. Really, I am. Go on then," I urged, praying he wouldn't come any closer. But his approach hastened toward me, much to my dismay.

"You don't look well, at all." Just as he was within inches of me, I sat back down.

"Bradley, you're missing out on educating yourself in the art of developing photographs. I'm a grown man, and I can take care of myself. Now please go," I said sharply, thoroughly losing my patience with him.

"Fine, have it your way. I'm only trying to help out a comrade."

"I know, and I appreciate it. I truly do. You're a good friend. I just need a minute to regain myself is all. See what you want to see, and let's get out of here."

Finally, he turned and entered the room where the old man was, closing the door behind him. As soon as the door clicked shut, I quickly got up and decided at once that I must dispose of the blood-smudged pillow. But how? Without much time to think the situation through, I hurried for the coatrack. I swiftly unhooked my coat and threw it on. This did not help in my quest to cool off. The nervous perspiration was not only dripping from my forehead, but was now forming a puddle between my breasts.

I turned my attention to the chair once again and decided that if I could place the cushion underneath my coat, I might be able to get away from the unfortunate incident unscathed and undetected. I reached for the cushion and tugged slightly on it, realizing quickly that it was tied to the back of the chair.

"No, no…" I muttered under my breath, tugging on it again with no luck. And it was luck that I needed presently. The other unfortunate part of this was that I could hear them talking behind the closed door, and it sounded like they were about to come out.

I pulled at the cushion once more, but to no avail. Their voices were becoming louder as they approached the door. My heart beat uncontrollably as I yanked and jerked at the damn thing, but it was still unwilling to budge. My brain ran through one horrible scenario after another. "Come on. Please!" I pulled as hard as I could, attempting to rip the tie. Thinking of ways to undo this cushion, I finally grabbed for the dagger inside my uniform jacket, unsheathed it from its scabbard, and just as I was about to sever the tie, the door opened. I pulled while I cut, and as they reentered the room, I shoved the pillow inside my long coat.

"Melvin, get a load of these," Bradley said as he came toward me, his arm outstretched with the photographs in his hands. I had closed my frock just in time, when he stood before me. "How are you feeling?"

With the stained cushion safely beneath my garments, I answered, "I'm feeling much better now. Whatever it was seems to have passed."

I wanted to look over the freshly developed pictures, but knew we needed to get out of there promptly before the old man noticed the missing pillow.

"They came out nicely, didn't they? Maybe we should take another."

I barely let him get his last word out before rushing him out the door, yelling behind me, "Thank you, sir."

Chapter Ten

I thought he would give me a hard time about not sitting for another picture, but his attention span was rather short, and once outside all was quickly forgotten. While we strolled over to the saloon, which was just a short distance from the photography shop, I contemplated how much blood was on the backside of my uniform trousers, and thanked God none had passed through to my coat. This was a real problem and needed to be resolved immediately. I had gotten my cycle several times since enlisting but had been fortunate enough to keep that to myself along with my true identity. The only person that could help me was Sadie. Sadie, whom I hoped was still speaking to me. It had been a month since I last saw her.

Bradley swung the saloon doors open and entered with me swiftly in tow. Like the first time we came, the stares and whispers were plentiful. We made our way through the tables and patrons, and moseyed up to the bar.

"Two shots," Bradley said loudly, slapping both of his hands down on the counter.

"None for me," I interjected before the barkeep poured the second shot.

"What? Why not?"

"Umm…my first time was my last time," I said, reminiscing of that night and the fact the room would not stop spinning. Regurgitating the alcohol was not the fun I had intended on, and the very thought of it burning its way down my throat was unappealing.

"A teetotaler, eh?"

"Call it what you will, my friend, but I will never drink liquor ever again in my life."

He shrugged his shoulders. "Suit yourself." He lifted his glass, tipped his head back, and opened his throat to receive the golden liquid.

While he talked incessantly, I scanned the room for Sadie. Glancing to my left, I saw a few tables filled with men, cards, and money. They were imbibing heavily and smoking cigars. A few women mingled with the gamblers, and the overall mood was a good one. Absent was Sadie. I peered over to my right where the piano player struck the keys, an elegantly dressed lady singing a tune beside him. I surveyed the dancing couples one by one until I eventually came across her.

She was dancing with an older gentleman, smiling and laughing as she twirled and circled the floor with him. I tried my darndest to draw her attention. Even as I stood there, I could feel the warm blood running down my thigh. I needed her help desperately. I prayed that my uniform trousers weren't drenched in blood, and thanked God for the long frock coat that hid all.

I was relieved when Bradley started conversing with the gent next to us. Keeping him entertained was exhausting, for his high spiritedness was unmatched. My eyes were quickly averted back to Sadie, who was still dancing and oblivious to my presence. Each time her face turned in my direction, I attempted to gain her attention. By the time her eyes connected with mine, I was back to an all-out sweat with beads of perspiration forming on my forehead once more. I smiled. She snubbed me, glaring at me before turning away. I was mortified. If she didn't help me, I was clueless as to what my next move would be. I feared for my imminent discovery, so each time her dance partner spun her my way, I tried my best to regather her attention. This time, there was no smile on my part, only panic. When she saw it, she too looked panicked and stricken with fear. She excused herself graciously from the man she was dancing with. In his drunken stupor, he reluctantly let her go. She headed for the staircase.

I wasn't sure of her intent and waited patiently by the bar, scoping her every stride. When she reached the steps, she turned to find me in the crowd. A simple nod to me indicated I had permission to follow. I looked around and swallowed hard, knowing once I moved, I must move hurriedly, having no protection and nowhere else for the blood to go but down. Praying I didn't leave a small trail of blood behind me, I swiftly separated myself from Bradley, and as nonchalantly as I could, sauntered to the stairs and followed her up.

"What is it? Are you feeling ill?" She interrogated me as soon as she shut the door behind us.

Her bedroom seemed different somehow this time. Last time, it was tense with anxiety over a romp in the pillows with a woman unaware that I was a woman, too. This time, her knowledge of my truth made it feel more like a safe haven.

Straightforward and to the point, I blurted out, "I have my female monthly. It came on out of nowhere, and I only found out when I got up from a cushioned chair. Look." I pulled the stained cushion from my coat.

Her face was somber and serious as she said, "It's all right. I can discard this inconspicuously. You don't have to be so frightened."

"It's not that I'm frightened of. It's this." I removed my coat and turned around.

Her face was aghast as she sucked in air swiftly. Her eyes widened and she covered her mouth with her hand. "Oh, dear."

"What am I to do?" My panic rose as I saw hers.

She dashed to the closet and began rifling through her own garments. "Sadie, what on earth are you doing?" I asked while my patience progressively thinned.

"Hold on," she said, raising her hand to quiet me.

"But Sadie…" Her head popped out of the cluster of dresses. She pulled from it a pair of Union Army trousers. "What the…Where did you get those?" I asked, amazed at how she just saved my hide. Or did she?

When she handed them to me, I lifted them up to get a better look at them. "Sadie," I exclaimed, and held them up directly in front of her. "These are enormous! Way too big for me. I'll drown in them."

"If you don't attempt to wear them, they'll drown you," she reminded me.

I looked over them once more, discerning any way I could possibly take them in. "I don't have the time, or the tools, to alter these, and even if I did, I don't think I could. They're entirely too big. Where did you get them?" I asked once again.

"A customer, so to speak. But in the morning, while he still lay asleep in my bed, Clifford T. Booker barged into my room and threw a bucket of water on him. Clifford loathes Yankee soldiers, and chased him clear out into the street in nothing but his underwear. He's lucky it was summer at the time."

"Truly? Well, where is this Clifford T. Booker now?" I asked, slightly concerned.

"He hates Yankees so much, he made northwest into Missouri to join the guerilla forces of William Quantrill. He and his band of outlaws harass and kill Union forces and sympathizers along the Missouri-Kansas border."

"Dear God." I dragged my fingers through my hair. "I pray I never run into him."

Such as it was, my situation had not changed since seeking Sadie's help. "What am I going to do?" I asked dejectedly, and threw the pants on her bed, giving up hope of my clandestine plan of living as a man. Once found out, I had no idea of what would become of me, what penalties, if any, I would be made to endure. I was uneasy that I would not walk away unscathed.

"Don't despair. I have a plan," she said, and picked the trousers back up. Her brain formulated a story right before me, and after providing me with rags to place between my legs, she helped put the large pantaloons on me. Foregoing any real time together, we set her plan in motion.

"Get out!" she yelled, and yelled loudly. "You Yankees are mannerless. How dare you suggest such lewd acts? Get out!"

I scrambled to the door, holding the pants up above my waist, and scurried out with half my coat on and half off. She pushed me out the door, yelling louder and more obnoxiously in an effort to draw attention from the other bedrooms.

"I don't want your money, I just want you out, Billy Yank."

As men and women alike came out of their rooms to see what was the bustle, I yelled back. "But these aren't even my pants! Give me back my britches, at once."

"Be thankful you are not naked, and leave."

It was just my good fortune that when I turned to leave, there was Bradley, having come out of an adventuress' bedchamber to see the chaos.

"You heard the lady, Billy. Get to moving," a Southern man said, defending Sadie in her unknown hoax. "Go on, Billy. Get!" He taunted me, shooing me away and directing me to depart.

Bradley quickly grabbed me by the scruff of my coat, and led me down the steps and out the doors. I was saved!

"What was that all about?" Bradley asked, baffled by the scene that had just transpired and the spectacle made inside.

The sun had made its descent and the temperature had dropped, leaving a frigid chill in the air. I couldn't button my coat because I had to hold my britches up. So, with one hand I held the waist of my trousers, and with the other held one side of my coat over my chest, trying to protect myself from the wind.

"I don't want to talk about it," I said, attempting to cut this conversation short.

"No, no. She said you asked her to do something unspeakable. Good God, what was it?"

"It's none of your business, and I'd rather not discuss it. I'm embarrassed and ashamed, and need to apologize to her soon."

"Did you ask her to stick it in her arse? Come on, Melvin, confess the corn already," he said while laughing wickedly.

"Bradley, stop," I yelled, not appreciating his boorishness. "It is not necessary to speak so crassly of a woman."

"She's hardly a lady," he said, pointing out her ways of prostitution and immorality. When I didn't answer, he made an attempt to lighten the mood. "Listen, don't go marrying this one. She's all used up."

At that, I gave him one good shove, surprising him and sending him falling to the ground. His behind skidded across the gravel of the dirt road, and when he came to a stop, he glanced up at me in dismay.

"Melvin, what in God's name has gotten into you?"

"I warned you to stop speaking so coarsely of her. Your insolence is completely unnecessary no matter what her occupation or station in life. I won't stand for it any longer."

"For a young boy, you've got an awful lot of nerve." He lifted himself up, challenging me. "Do you care to duel?"

"Don't be ridiculous." I offered my hand to him, helping him up the rest of the way.

"Remind me not to anger you again. And next time, aim that anger at the Rebels, not me."

We snickered at each other's behavior, and he joked, "But if you do, you'll need both hands." He laughed and pointed to the enormous trousers I still clutched. The mood lightened as he handed me a pinch of snuff, and we continued our footslog to camp.

When we arrived, I went straight to the Quartermaster for a new pair of uniform pants. By myself,

I walked back to our quarters. There were a few privates milling about, so I kept my frock coat on while I changed, using great caution to keep the rag in place between my thighs. Once in pantaloons that fit me more accurately, I settled to my usual level of apprehension. Today had taught me a valuable lesson. Keeping my true identity in the shadows was turning out to be much more difficult than previously thought.

Chapter Eleven

In came the new year, 1863, and with it much news. A battle was fiercely fought 235 miles from where we sat in Memphis. A town called Murfreesboro and a river called Stones were the scene of a costly Union victory. General William Rosecrans freed middle Tennessee from Rebel control and boosted Northern morale. It was wonderful news, but only made us realize how stagnant our company as a whole division had become. We wanted to fight. We wanted to support our fellow soldiers already in the midst and thick of things.

The bigger news was receiving word that on New Year's Day, President Lincoln made effective his Emancipation Proclamation, freeing those slaves in Rebel territories. The men's opinions were mixed on the subject. Some of my favorite comrades despised the idea of freeing the black man and making him equal to the white man. When I asked one man why, then, he was fighting for the Union Army, he replied, "What choice did I have? I am from the North, and my father would have disowned me for sure had I not. I did not know the president would make this war about slavery. However, he has. But to say I like darkies? No, I do not."

Others didn't think the president went far enough in his proclamation, suggesting that he did not outlaw slavery altogether. "Tis a national sin, and it is up to us to dismantle the institution of slavery from our land. I am a believer in the Declaration of Independence that says all men are created equal. There is no one that can convince me that one man may rightfully make another man his slave," said an abolitionist soldier sitting across from me, pushing his half-eaten meal away from him.

The discussion became intensely heated between several of the men, and in the end, a bunch of us had to break up some fisticuffs exchanged between them. When I grabbed the arm of one of the burlier men, he practically dragged me with him each time he socked the man in front of him. Ted, seeing my struggle, came to aid me in restraining him. After a few choice profanities were exchanged, things settled down.

⁂

I allowed a few weeks to pass before I had the courage to show my face in town again. When I entered the saloon, I averted my eyes from any attention that may possibly come my way. This was the first time I had come into town by myself, and I was nervous to say the least. I prayed no one would recognize me, but the Lord didn't see it that way. "Ain't you that Yankee feller that wanted to perform lewd acts on Sadie?" asked a gray-haired gentleman, his face replete with scraggly whiskers. His eyes burned a hole through me as his brows came together, leaving a deep wrinkle in his forehead.

"Yes, sir. I've come to apologize," I quietly replied.

"Speak up, son." He countered my softness with harshness.

Realizing I needed to show some confidence in an environment that called for it, I spoke up with vigor. "Sir! Yes, sir. I've come to apologize to the lady, as I've seen the error of my ways."

"I reckon Sadie doesn't want to see you."

"Perhaps, but nonetheless, I'd like to try."

Before he could halt my progress, Sadie appeared before me.

"I see you've come to humble yourself," she said saucily.

"Indeed, I have."

"I think I've written off you Northern soldiers, crude as you are." She played the part genuinely, as if our quarrel was that of reality. I, myself, almost fell for her ploy.

"I'd really like to make things right, miss." I tipped my hat in sincerity.

With a slight smirk of the twisted corner of her mouth, she took my hand and led me away from the man still scowling at me. "You holler if you need assistance, Sadie. I'll fill the bastard full of holes," he said, looking me up and down in complete disgust.

Each creak of the floorboards beneath my boots drew unwanted attention I could not afford. Stares and whispers came from various men and women fraternizing in the hallway. However, once inside the safety of her bedchamber, I finally breathed a sigh of relief.

"How are you?" she asked, happy to see me. "Can you stay for a bit? No calamity this time, I presume?" She stroked my arm with her hand. The smile in her eyes contained a sensuous flame.

"No calamities today. Spending time with you would do my heart good. I would love to partake in some good conversation." I started, took her hand from my arm, and placed it in mine. "I am eternally grateful to you, Sadie. You saved, not only my identity, but my life as well. I'm indebted to you tenfold." A gleam and sparkle shined from her eyes with an expression of adoration. "Why do you look at me so?" I asked, raising my hand to her face and brushing over her cheek with featherlight strokes. "Your want of a man surely must be superior to your want of me, yes?" I was surprised by her flirtatiousness after discovering I was actually a woman.

"A man doesn't possess the sensitivity that you do, and since all believe you are a man, I believe I shall indulge in those much-desired qualities. I've not yet been able to let go of the memory of your touch." Her fingertips caressed my lips before her mouth replaced them. My eyes gently shut as I delighted in the warmth and softness of her full lips. I welcomed her kiss and she moved closer to me, eventually leaving no space between us. Her breasts pressed up against my bound bosom, and she wrapped her arms around my neck, sinking into the closeness we shared. Her femininity intoxicated me, making my head flighty and dizzy, my groin suddenly on fire with lust.

"This isn't much like talking," I said, certain that was all that would take place today.

"Is that what you would prefer?" She mocked me playfully, her lips leaving mine only to utter her brief words.

The tingling in my lower half took control of my mouth, and I found myself replying, "My preference is to lay you upon this bed."

"Then do so before I come to my common sens-es."

No more words were necessary as I guided her onto the feather mattress, laying her on her back and placing my own body atop hers. The more aroused I became, the more I squirmed, my pelvis involuntarily thrusting forward on hers. My mouth hungered for her, and I kissed and suckled my way over her throat, lifting her blouse out of and above her skirt to fondle her breasts. Her heavy breathing indicated her own arousal as she pressed her lips against my own neck, urgent to taste the saltiness of each other's delicate skin.

We rolled around on the bed together, tangled up in one another's embrace. I ended up on my back with her straddling me and dangling her lovely breasts in my face. I teased them with my mouth, suckling each before feeling her hand maneuver its way to my trousers. She started to take them down, and I abruptly stopped her advance. "What are you doing?" I asked, confused by her brazenness.

"I'm curious," she whispered into my ear.

But as I was about to allow her into my private garden, suddenly, *Pop! Pop! Pop!* Gunshots were let off downstairs, and we both jumped, startled from the loud noise. Heavy footsteps came up the steps, and a loud, raucous, hoarse voice yelled out, "Sadie Rose."

"Oh my," Sadie said.

"What? Who is it?" My own fear escalated from her tone of despair.

"It's Clifford."

"Clifford who?" But even as I spoke the name out loud, I recalled her story of the Yankee-hating rogue who had taken up with guerilla raiders in killing Union soldiers.

"Clifford T. Booker." She shivered.

"Well, what's he doing here, and what's he want with you?"

"He liked me best amongst the other girls," she said, seemingly shaken by the very thought of him. "He's coming to my room. You must hide."

I hurriedly buttoned my britches in a state of panic and terror, and swiftly hid in the only place I could: her closet. The heavy trod of his boots moved closer and closer, and I stood buried in the lot of her dresses and garments.

With a swoosh, the door swung open quickly, forcefully hitting the wall with a thick thud and vibration. Enter a stocky, brawny man standing near six feet tall. His broad shoulders and mere height were intimidating enough, but factor in his gruff face with his piercing black eyes that were set in a permanent scowl, and fear was instantly instilled in my soul. His black eyes matched his long, pitch-black hair, straggly as it was. The stubble of his facial hair was thick and sporadic, unkempt. The clothes he wore were tattered and filthy, no more than qualifying as rags. His holster, strapped to his waist, held two Colt pistols, and drew most of my attention.

He slammed the door behind him, and in his heavy boots strode across the room toward Sadie. "Sadie Rose," he simply said, dragging his tongue across his lips and then the gap in his teeth, salivating for her as a wild animal would prior to attacking its prey. He took off his gun holster and laid it on the bed before grabbing her by the hips and pulling her to him.

"I thought you were off fighting the Yankees? What brings you back to town?" she asked while squirming under his grip that had now moved to her buttocks.

"My mother's been ill. Seems she won't recover. Came to say good-bye. Headed out tomorrow to meet up with the rest of the gang. Plannin' somethin' big." He grunted.

The fight for Kansas had been an ongoing and bloody ordeal between guerilla raiders, who were pro-slavery, and the jayhawkers, who were anti-slavery. The debate on whether Kansas would enter the Union as a free or slave state had been heated. When it officially entered as a free state, the guerillas wouldn't let it rest. They were a fierce bunch, with hatred in their hearts. But none of that mattered currently, as Clifford was about to take what he came for before returning to his posse of immoral heathens.

He expected no further conversation from her as he opened her blouse and roughly groped her breasts. I peeked out from between her garments in the closet, repulsed by what I saw. She agonized under his touch, visibly opposed to the action that was about to take place. While he handled her tender bosom, he bore his mouth onto her neck, eliciting a groan only from him.

However, when he turned her around, lifted her skirt, dropped her bloomers, and bent her over her dresser, I could no longer watch. I sank back into the pile of clothes, disgusted by his aggressiveness. "All I ask is that you not spill your seed inside of me," Sadie pitifully requested, preparing for the inevitable.

"I know the rules," he said with condescension in his voice.

I leaned forward, careful not to make a sound, and glimpsed through the dresses once more. My whole body shook with fear as I watched for the first time a man take a woman, though in this fashion I could hardly call it anything other than that. He savagely penetrated her, giving rise to a sharp and intense yelp from her throat. He was hurting her. But this wasn't about her. He cared so little for her that he didn't bother to undress, or even take down his britches. He used his manhood as a ramrod with no feeling or concern for her arousal or pleasure. She was simply a vessel for his human gratification.

I wanted to help her, to burst forth from the closet and beat him the way a man beats another man with fists. But I knew I would be no contest for his stalwart strength, and I feared he would kill us both. I caught a gander of the pistols still in their holster lying on the bed. Had they not been in the holster, I may have had a chance to leap at them and take aim, but luck would not be on my side that day. Giving up hope of aiding her in her distress, I receded back into the depths of her dark closet, sinking back into the heap of soft garments. I covered my ears and prayed for God to end her torment.

The few minutes it took for him to finish his manly business felt like an eternity, but with a low guttural groan he buttoned his trousers, strapped his holster back around his waist, and headed for the door. Before he left, he threw his payment for services on her end table, then departed her bedchamber.

As the door clicked shut, I sprang from the closet to her side. She wept uncontrollably as she rebuttoned her blouse. My heart hurt for her, and I reached for her, taking her into my arms and embracing her. Watching and listening to her be violated by a beast of a man made me want to comfort her, but I didn't know how. She could speak no words as she failed in her attempt to choke back her tears.

I led her to the bed, laid her gently upon it, and climbed in with her. I cradled her as she rested her head on my flattened bosom and vented her sadness. There was nothing for me to say, no words that could make it better. I swept her disheveled hair away from her eyes and kissed her forehead. Although I was not in love with her, I cared deeply for her and longed to end her days of prostitution, to end her strife in being demeaned and used by men. There was no longer any playful teasing of one another. And to be quite frank, we never sought physical intimacy again.

Each time I returned to see her, we merely lay in her bed, held each other, and discussed our pasts and what we dreamed for the future. The intimacy we shared was an emotional one, caring for one another in ways no one else could. She shared with me her dreams of owning property someday, and of doing something different with her life. This had been what she wanted in return for her silence in keeping my identity: property. She had been squirreling away what money she could in hopes of purchasing land someday, however, women could not purchase or own property. These transactions were only made between men, and such was my position as it stood. No one knew me from around here, so I didn't have to be concerned with locals finding out.

We made no plans for the purchase of said property, or at least not yet. The reality that I was part of a war that was going on all around us was lost on me whenever I was with Sadie. Her fondness of me was evident in her smile and obvious adoration. She desired a man who was kind to her, who loved her. I reminded her that I was not that man. No matter her affection, underneath my uniform was still a woman. And what she desired was the gentleness of a man, not a woman.

"Who's to say?" she would ask. "I like the feel of your touch. And although you are not a man, you certainly live as one."

"True enough. But even if I had that kind of affection for you, I'm a soldier, ready to march at the given order."

She nodded her head in understanding, and our friendship flourished and grew. Spending time with her while off duty helped pass the mundane time at the fort. Little did we know our time together would soon end. Talk of troop movement was rampant around camp, and the excitement of the boys was uncontainable.

Chapter Twelve

Guard duty was boring, and a task I dreaded most. Tonight, it was my turn to keep watch over part of the perimeter of the fort. Protecting my comrades as they slept was a priority, and staying awake and alert was necessary. I was the sentry posted on the opposite side of the river. It was the southwestern part of the fort, and most prone to being attacked. It couldn't withstand another naval fight. I relieved the sentry who had been there the last couple of hours, set my rifle on my shoulder, and walked my post. A thirty-yard march back and forth was my duty for the next two hours, until I was relieved by a fresh guard.

It was midnight, and the only light shining was that of the brightly lit stars in the pitch-black sky. It was the beginning of March, and there was a crisp chill in the night air. My breath was visible each time I exhaled, and without letting my weapon touch the ground I buttoned my coat to the top of my neck. I trod from one tree and back to the other. It was dark beyond the few trees directly in my line of sight, yet I glimpsed something racing and dodging through the woods. It caused me to come to port arms and challenge it. "Halt!" Realizing it was only an animal passing by, I never finished my command and reshouldered my weapon. Each breaking branch that I heard was cause for investigation, always ending in it being a deer or racoon.

All was fairly quiet until about one o'clock, when a horse came galloping across the terrain, and I, not knowing if the rider was friend or foe, came to the ready and called out, "Halt! Who goes there?"

"Friend," said the mystery rider as he came to a stop about twenty feet from me. Finally, I could see the blue Union uniform. His long jacket was single-breasted with shoulder straps.

But still, I had to verify without letting him in range of my bayonet. "Halt, friend. Advance with the countersign."

He rode closer at a slow pace, and when he was within earshot of me, he leaned down from his steed and whispered, "Shiloh. I'm Lieutenant Peter Farley, aide-de-camp to General Weaver with orders for General Cox."

With his countersign being correct, I let him pass to the next post closer to the entrance of the fort. My heart was slow to quiet, for it was beating out of control. Anytime a horse and rider came galloping your way as you stood guard, your level of apprehension was more than great.

❧ ❧ ❧ ❧

Again, I marched between my marked trees, back and forth, keeping watch through the darkness of night as best I could. Time passed by without further incident. But then, with a rustle of some leaves on the ground and the snapping of some fallen branches, I became uneasy, and explored a possible situation. I crept up to a thicket of pines and oaks, peering left and right, but didn't see anything out of the ordinary.

A little bit deeper into the woods, where a fog settled, I heard footsteps ruffle the leaves again. Someone was present and not wanting me to know. However, it was my job to know, so I patrolled in the direction of the disturbance. Scanning the area, I squinted hard, attempting to see through the murk.

Snap! went a broken branch just to the right of me. I wheeled that way, my weapon at the ready. "Halt! Who goes there?" No response came. Again, I yelled out, "Halt! Who goes there?" Again, no response was had. Before I called for the Corporal of the Guard, I cocked the trigger of my rifle and ordered, "You're best to come out of the shadows, and into my view, before I blow your goddammed head off!" Cursing was not in my repertoire, but angst had set in, and feeling threatened put me on high alert.

"Please, don't shoot!" came a faceless voice from the depths of obscurity.

"Come forward so I can see you, and step slowly now."

"Please, sir. My family and me be on da run," a man said as he cautiously approached me with his hands held high. A black man, clearly a runaway slave, sank to his knees before me. All I could see of him was the wide whites of his eyes and his teeth as he spoke. The fear in his stare made me ill at ease. I had never before spoken to a negro, let alone a slave.

"Stand up and come into the light of the moon," I said, and as he stood and stepped forward, I examined his condition. His clothes, or rather, rags, were tattered and scraggy. His feet were bare, scathed with cuts and wounds from treading across the sticks and backwoods on his way to anticipated and desperate freedom. I asked, "Where you from?" My bayonet was still aimed toward him.

"Mississippi, sir. Massa says he tendin' to sell me off without my family. I got four children. Massa done sold my two little ones. But I has my other two here," he said, and brought his two children out of the darkness. I could barely understand his vernacular, but listened intently nonetheless. He continued. "Massa done whipped my wife near to death. Just on a counta she cried for her children." His wife then appeared from a thicket of bushes, bruised, beaten, and lacerated from a lashing.

I could not believe my eyes. When I reached out to examine her wounds, she cowered away from me. "You made it all this way without being detected?" I asked.

"Yessa," he replied, and took his wife in his arms as his two remaining children clung to his leg and waist. His daughter appeared to be about the age of ten, his son about five. The panic and terror painted across their faces pulled at my heart. They were pathetic, wretched creatures, and my pity fell on them, but I wasn't sure what to do.

"Sir, we just want be free. We hear Union soldiers is helpin' black folk out of the South. I'm hopin' you'll help me and my family."

His children trembled, scared to death of a white man in military attire. If they only knew. "I don't mean to frighten any of you, but I must make a formal call to the corporal, so that he may help," I said, before calling out, "Corporal of the Guard!"

Immediately, the corporal dashed from his post to mine. Once there, he looked as befuddled as I when he saw the family. He picked up his kepi and scratched his head. "What exactly do we have here,

Private Coffield?"

"Runaways from Mississippi, sir."

He surveyed them from head to toe, then ordered, "Come with me." He guided them in the direction of the fort and disappeared from sight. Like it or not, Union lines had become safe havens for what the other men called "runaway contraband." I found the term dehumanizing, but it was a word that was bandied about freely. The newly freed men and women did everything they could to stay within those lines. The men cut wood, loaded and unloaded supplies, some drove transportation wagons, and the women cooked and washed clothes.

My shift now over for the next six hours, my relief sentry appeared, gave me the countersign, and took my position. I scampered off toward my sleep quarters with horrible images of that colored woman's bruises, and the sight of the raw wounds strewn across her back. I could not fathom living her life, if life is what I should call it. The very thought of being sold off to another man without my family filled me with faithlessness and disbelief. When I looked into that woman's eyes, I saw a soul there. A human soul filled with pain, sorrow, and hopelessness. All the things I felt when I left my family farm. But no one sold me, or forced me to leave. I wasn't anyone's property. They were. I could not accept this truth, this despicable institution. It was in this instance that I realized I, too, was an abolitionist. I must be, for I agreed with all that they stood for. Freedom should be for everyone, and I would lay my life down for it if need be.

My heart was choked by the overwhelming emotion of mankind, and how some folks possessed the empathy needed to be decent and some did not.

Some insisted that their superiority came from treating others as inferior. White men were so threatened by the negro that they found it necessary to treat him as less than themselves, to overpower him, to show his authority over what he considered to be an untamed animal. These wealthy Southern men used and abused these people. Working them at hard labor from sunrise until sunset. Breeding them like dogs so that they may use and abuse their offspring, and then sell them off one at a time, separating families forever sometimes.

I crawled into my bunk and tried to erase the images that flashed through my mind. It should have been easy to fall asleep, as I was physically and mentally exhausted, but sleep would not come. As restless as I was, it took a while before my eyes finally shut, knowing it would be my turn, in just a few short hours, to stand guard once again.

⁂

The second week of March brought with it warmer temperatures and news that we would be marching out of Memphis soon. There was no time to see Sadie and bid her farewell. This saddened me, but my priority was serving the Army, and serving it well. Performing in drill with distinction and going above and beyond in every task I undertook finally warranted me a promotion to corporal. Two sky-blue stripes now donned the sleeves of my uniform jacket.

I wished to share my good news with Sadie, who had become a dear friend to me. But again, there was no time and no permission given for leaving the fort until we marched out to head southward. I sat on a tree stump I used to cut the men's hair and proceeded to write a letter to Sadie. I informed her of my inevitable departure, not knowing when—nor even if—I would ever see her again. However, I vowed to her that if I got out of this war alive, I would be back to help her obtain the property she so dreamed of. And I meant it.

⁂

While ending my correspondence, a bustle filled with excitement came from the center of the fort, not far from where I sat. I sprang from the stump and ran the distance to a grouping of tents that housed a regiment of men, temporarily, on their way through to other destinations. When I arrived upon the scene, a crowd of men were gathered around one tent in particular. Screaming could be heard from within. The screaming wasn't the peculiar part of it, though, but that it was a female's scream, high in pitch and tone.

I forced my way through the circle of men, wiggling and pushing others aside to get a good look. When I finally reached the entrance of the tent, a young soldier popped out, his face pale with surprise. "Well, what is it, man?" I asked, my curiosity getting the better of me.

He scanned the group of soldiers anxiously awaiting his answer, and then he looked at me. "It would seem to me that Private Pettit is giving birth!"

"Pardon me?" I didn't believe I heard him correctly, so I asked him to repeat himself.

"It's difficult to understand, I know. But Private Pettit is having a baby!"

I could not believe my ears. "A baby?"

"Yes, a baby."

"Oh dear!" I cringed, and hoped no one noticed my insecurities. Gathering my courage, I stepped forward, opened the flap of the tent, and peeked inside. A woman that resembled me—disguised as a man—was wearing the top half of a blue Union uniform. The bottom half had been discarded and her legs were wide open. A baby's head protruded from her birth canal, and within moments, with one last scream, she pushed the child all the way out.

I backed away from the scene slowly. I felt as though everyone was staring at me, as if they somehow knew I was a fraud. The talking and whispering that took place of this newfound information was directed at the tent, however I felt as though they were speaking of me. Panic-stricken, and with beads of perspiration now forming on my brow, I turned and weaved my way back through the crowd and away from said tent. As I did, the infant cried out its first voice of life. A miracle and a curse all at once. Another female posing as a man was cause for concern for me.

Far-fetched ideas of everyone being stripped down to detect any other women in our ranks ran uncontrollably through my mind. Paranoia set in. I couldn't get away from the scene fast enough, and double-quicked to my company's quarters. Once inside and without any intention, I broke down in tears. I climbed up onto my bunk and buried my face in my pillow, refusing to allow any of my comrades to see me. There were others in the room playing a friendly round of checkers. Others were reading the Bible, or some other form of book. And some wrote letters to their loved ones. At this I sobbed even harder, stuffing my face further in the pillow in an attempt to stifle my sorrow.

The reality of being an orphan, of being alone, truly alone in this world, finally broke me. I felt the same loneliness that drove me here and to my current situation. I allowed myself this good cry, knowing I must find my courage again to move forward in my life. After some time, I eventually drifted into sleep.

"Melvin, wake up," Ted shouted, shaking my leg in an effort to rouse me from my slumber. "Private Pettit just gave birth!"

"I already know. I was there," I said, and rolled back over.

"No. I mean to tell you, they've taken her, the father, and the infant to stockade."

"The father?" I mused.

"Yes, Sergeant Pettit. Everyone thought they were brothers. Turns out, they're man and wife. She didn't want to be left at home without him, so she chose to disguise herself as a man to enlist with him." He gave me a knowing look, maybe feeling a bit uneasy for my own welfare.

"Oh, Heavens! Why were they brought to the stockade?"

"Melvin, a woman cannot legally enlist in the Army."

"What is her punishment to be?" Anguish coated my tone.

"I don't know. But for now, that's where they are."

This disturbed me more. The idea of not only getting caught, but being jailed for it, was more than upsetting. I questioned my decision to carry on this charade. Worse, I was informed I would be part of the guard detail watching over them.

However, before I stood watch, Sergeant Pettit

was released back to his unit with nothing more than a light punishment of wearing a placard around his neck announcing his crime. It read, *My cowardice is such that I needed my wife to hold my hand.* He was demoted all the way back to private. The other fellows laughed and made fun of him. But I was more worried about his wife's fate.

How bizarre that I should stand guard over a woman whose crime was my own! Before I started my shift, I peeked inside the small room where we were keeping her. She sat in a chair by the window, feeding her baby through her breast. She swaddled the babe, clearly bonding with her child. It was sweet to witness, but this was no place for them. I struggled with her possible punishment as though it were mine.

As luck would have it, within a few days she and her newborn were sent home. No further punishment was doled out, and although I was not her, I was grateful for the outcome. Amongst the other men, I watched as the horse and carriage drove them off. The boys made fun and joked about having a female in their ranks and no one being the wiser for it. Apparently, she had been in their ranks since their regiment was mustered in at the onslaught of war.

Chapter Thirteen

Aweek and a half more passed before our company packed our gear and supplies, and departed Fort Pickering. We lined up in columns of two and began our march. We left Memphis, Company B, 93rd Indiana Infantry, 3rd Brigade, 8th Division, 16th Army Corp. We were proud and we were ready. Ready to fight! We were a green regiment, but our spirit was enthusiastic and eager. We wanted to be in the thick of battle. We wanted to do our part. We also understood that we were needed in an attempt to aid General Grant, who endeavored several expeditions in an effort to gain and hold Vicksburg, Mississippi. His attempts failed, but giving up was not an option.

Vicksburg was located high on a bluff on the Mississippi River overlooking a horseshoe-shaped bend in the river. Natural defenses of the city were optimal, making it the Gibraltar of the Confederacy. It was critical in sending supplies and men up and down, and the closest to the Confederate's main supply route from New Orleans. The Union had closed in on and held the fortifications the Rebels occupied up and down the Mississippi. Vicksburg was the last stronghold and what kept the South's two halves together. Without this city, the Confederates would be choked, nearly to death.

We left Memphis and crossed the Mississippi River by naval vessels transporting soldiers from east to west. As we landed in Arkansas, our march started off robustly. We were all filled with anticipation of the unknown. However, after fifteen miles, we began to lag. I, for one, was tired. My legs felt like sandbags, and my feet were sore. The others didn't seem to be faring much better. As the men in front slowed, so did the rest of us, and avoiding the man in front of you became impossible. It was a warm day for the end of March and all I desired to do was take off my jacket, but suffer I must. Perspiration seeped down my face, and I was compelled to whisk it away with my sleeve only to have it build up to be dried again. I repeated this action all the way to our first bivouac somewhere in the bottomland wilderness. With not enough rest, and just before dawn, we marched again. We marched twenty miles a day. It took us five days through uncharted territory to get to Helena, a town set on the Mississippi River. Wealthy cotton plantations lined the river where we bivouacked for the rest of daylight and the night. We hadn't stopped to eat, or even urinate, in miles worth of walking. The men were more than exhausted, having never walked this far from anywhere.

With much-needed rest had, we began our march from Helena back into the wilderness, where there were no roads or even trails. We climbed over rocks and tread through canals of water that led to the river. It was muddy and messy, and physically draining, all of us bogged down with a loaded haversack and musket. Moss-draped cypress trees loomed above us as we weaved our way down the delta. We were tough, but our progress lagged as the terrain became dense and almost impassable. We set up camp, no rest available as we still needed to establish our perimeters, erect our tents, and start our campfires. Everyone needed to eat, including the horses, and our temporary camp was a bustle of activity getting the necessaries accomplished.

Ted and I were still bunk mates. Setting up our tents in circles, we claimed our spot. I pulled from my haversack my half of our pup tent, and Ted retrieved his half to complete our temporary housing for the night. Once constructed, we all went to cooking our meals over the fire. Ted and I fried some salted pork in a pan. We added crumbled hard tack and fried them with our pork and bacon fat, a dish Union soldiers called skillygalee. To say it was tasty would be a downright lie, but we consumed it anyway. How we would crave this meal in the near future.

We slept for a short time, and before dawn brewed our coffee and got to packing up our tents and gear. At six o'clock, we formed lines of marchers and headed deeper into the South another twenty miles, and closer to our destination to meet up with General Grant. It took us nearly all of the month of April to get there. We were on the bend of one of many bayous, and the temperature was warm enough as the sun beat down its rays that men shed their uniforms and jumped in the still-frigid water. Most of the men just wanted to bathe. A few couldn't take the cold, brown, cedar-like water and immediately got out, chicken skin covering their whole body as they ran for the warmth of their uniforms. Others thrived around, splashing and laughing, the cold water making them feel like they were alive.

"Come on in, Melvin," Bradley exclaimed, inviting me into this romp of wet men.

"I couldn't." I was tired of coming up with plausible excuses, but this one seemed reasonable enough, even if it would mean another onslaught of teasing. "It's too cold."

"You get used to it. Come on, I'm positive you could use a bath just like the rest of us."

The sight of naked men repulsed me, and before he could beg me any further, I diverted into a thicket of woods. Staying to myself was something I attempted to do, but my comrades would not allow for that, insisting melancholy would set in and no soldier needed that. So, I took some much-needed time for myself. I missed Sadie, missed our talks and our closeness.

This was the first time since Memphis that I had a chance to even remotely think of her. Marching miles at a time, for hours a day, was mentally exhausting all in itself. My body was worn and tired. My feet felt swollen all the time from not enough rest, and my throat was dry and parched from rationing my water.

I pushed aside branches of trees to shimmy through, searching for what, I wasn't sure. I kept going though, knowing I couldn't go far from camp but needing to detach momentarily. Weaving through wild bushes and tall reeds of grass, I came across a small section of the bayou secluded from the rest of camp. My initial reaction was to undress and bathe away from the others. However, doubt and fear crept into my psyche and took up permanent residence there.

I looked to my right, surveying the thick woods for any sign of humans. Then, I took a gander to my left, searching for any movement through the foliage of trees. My sight connected with the brown, murky water once again. The warm air made it look appealing.

I hadn't bathed for a while as it was difficult to be alone in the midst of hundreds of men, all of whom bathed in front of one another. Opportunities were scarce for all, but for me it was damn near impossible.

Taking my uniform jacket off, I rolled up the sleeves of my shirt and ran my hand over my arm. The chalkiness of filth was caked to my skin at least two inches thick. I knelt down and splashed my fingers around in the water, ensuring the temperature was adequate. The water was indeed cold, but I was soiled with grime and muck. The water won.

Scanning the area one last time, I undressed quickly, taking from my pocket a bottle of fragrant oils as I did. I unbound my breasts and dipped a toe into the cedar-like water. I chattered, folding my arms across my breasts. Tiny bumps spread over my entire body as I submerged myself slowly into the pond. I doused myself in the oil and scrubbed my skin briskly. Bathing would have to be brief and curt so as not to draw any attention to my absence.

Cleanliness was a feeling like no other, a sensation of becoming five pounds lighter just by scouring off a thick coating of dirt. I scooped up the water, cupping it with my hands, and splattered it on my face repeatedly. Then, I plunged my head beneath the surface, sprang back up, and lathered the oil through my hair. Several more times I immersed my head below the surface, thoroughly rinsing it and my body.

Hastily, I climbed from the pond and pulled a small blanket from my haversack. Using it as a towel, I wiped myself down without delay. I was in such a hurry, I precipitately yanked my pants on, one leg at a time, tripping over my own feet. The only task I took great pains in undertaking was binding my bosom to my body, making sure my chest was as flat as possible. I finished dressing, combed my hair, and made my way out of the copse of trees.

ﺎﻠﻤﺔ

When I got back to camp, some of the men were busy cooking while others fell asleep where they stood, completely spent of all energy. I came across Bradley, who was taking a swig from his canteen. "Want some?" he asked, offering it to me with one hand and raking his fingers through his hair with the other.

I took the canteen from him, cocked my head back, and swallowed hard. I expected water, but instead recognized the taste as whiskey. I promptly sprayed and spit it from my mouth. "My Lord, Bradley," I exclaimed as I wiped my lips with the sleeve of my arm, my face scrunched up in distaste.

He laughed a hardy, jovial laugh and smacked me on the back, sending me forward a bit unbalanced. "Come now, Melvin. A small snort won't sufficiently hurt you."

"I told you I don't drink anymore."

"Oh, that's right, a teetotaler." He gushed condescendingly, taking a moment before retorting. "A teetotaler, my finger. You want to know when you'll drink again?"

"Never. I told you."

"When we get our first taste of battle."

"Battle?"

"We're close to Vicksburg. One final push through to Grant, and then onward to face the enemy."

I pondered the reality of his words. Battle. My

stomach became queasy, wondering if I would have the courage I swore I possessed. Truth be told, I was anxious and scared of what was unknown to me. Still, I was as prepared as I could be, having been trained in the most modern techniques of warfare. But the unknown...the unknown made my heart skip a beat out of sheer fear. In my mind I placed myself in the midst of battle, facing the enemy directly in front of me. The vision sent a chill down my spine. I was trepidatious, but I was also determined to find my lion's heart.

While I was deep in thought, I heard voices raised in anger over by one of the officer's tents. The bickering became intense as Bradley and I drew closer to the clamor. "I told you I wanted a trim. You balded me, you bastard!" the officer yelled as he ran his hand over his head while he peered into a small mirror. The more he looked, the more enraged he became.

The young soldier, still standing with scissors in his hand, appeared stunned. When the officer glowered from the mirror to the soldier, he knocked the scissors clear out of his hands. "Get out," he said to the young man, entirely annoyed by the bad haircut he just received. "You're useless."

The degraded young man hung his head and scurried away in a heated rush. Bradley giggled wildly, holding his belly as he did. The officer was not amused at being the brunt of Bradley's obvious entertainment, and started for him. However, I stepped in his way and interrupted. "I can fix it for you."

He came to a halt and stared at me in disbelief. "What did you say?" He straightened his back and rose above me.

I stood in his shadow and reiterated my

statement. "I can fix it."

He returned to the chair he was sitting in when he'd received his uneven cut, and waited patiently for me. I picked the scissors up from the ground, wiped the blades on my uniform, and turned back to the awaiting officer. A snip here, a snip there, and his hair, though short, was even. Without his permission, I reached for the straight razor, lathered up his face, and gave him a clean shave.

When all was finished, I handed him the mirror. "Well, well. I'll be damned to hell." A smile formed on his countenance. "I am a handsome devil, aren't I?" He paused and stared at me, wordlessly suggesting that I should answer him, so I did.

"Sir. Yes, sir."

"Yes, sir, what?" He examined me a snippet further, his sneer deepening as he did.

"Sir! Yes, sir! You are a handsome devil." I corrected myself at once.

He gleamed with a brutish delight, proud of his superiority over me. I would later learn that he was Brigadier General John Robert Frommer, a business owner from Chicago who won a popularity contest to gain his rank when he raised up a regiment of volunteers. He was close friends with the mayor of Chicago, William Emmett Dever, and had no previous military background. To my understanding, he had not a lick of common sense about him, either. He cared more about his appearance than his service responsibilities. Flaunting his chicken guts, the twisted gold braiding up and down an officer's sleeve seemed to concern him more than anything else.

His size was intimidating, a feature well received by his men. He had to stand at least six feet five inches tall, if not more. He was handsome, and he was well aware of it. The brown sugar color of his eyes shined a brilliant glow, flashing an enthusiasm his men wished he would focus more on them than just his uniform and hair. He had a slender frame with long arms and long legs.

The hair he was so adamant in keeping kempt was a light brown, cut to ear level in the back, parted on the side, and combed back into a smooth style. He wore a full mustache and hair under his bottom lip in the shape of an arrow. As long as he felt he looked good, he was lighthearted and good-natured. However, should he be disheveled in any way or feel humiliated in front of fellow officers, he became quite ill-tempered and liverish.

"From now on, you shall groom my hair and face. What is your name, soldier?" he asked as he placed his very fancy slouch hat on his head. The hat was fashioned with long, black ostrich plumes and a black rosette surmounted with the US Eagle embroidered in the center.

"Corporal Melvin A. Coffield, sir," I said loudly and clearly.

He liked that. He liked my moxie, and he liked my confidence. His grin grew wide and his laugh bellowed ostentatiously throughout our camp. He patted my shoulder affirmingly and granted my leave.

I walked away just as baffled as when I walked into the bizarre scene. Fortune would have it as such—that I'd no idea that approaching General Frommer would be a godsend in my very near future. It seemed I would have plenty of time to contemplate my life and its possible demise when I learned I would once again stand watch. What I would learn this evening was that evil pervaded our own ranks.

⁂

All were fast asleep as I made my way with the rest of the sentinels being marched to their guard posts. With only a lantern for my guide, I relieved the sentry already there. I watched him as he rambled away and back toward camp, holding him in my line of sight until he vanished into the pitch-black night. I examined my surroundings as far as I could. It was quiet, nay for an animal here and there. The only fear I had, besides running into a Rebel, was alligators. I had yet to deal with one, but had heard of other soldiers getting tangled up with them on our trek through the bayous of Louisiana.

The dark soil beneath my shoes was moist, muddying them from heel to toe. Prodding with each step, the squish of my boots in the muck was the sole sound keeping me awake and alert. It was a good thing, too, because my pacing was interrupted by approaching horses. Four uniformed men galloped up and came to a stop directly in front of me. The front man was the officer of the day, along with a noncommissioned officer and two other men.

Bringing my arms to port, I challenged the party. "Who goes there?"

The NCO answered, "Grand rounds."

"Halt, grand rounds. Advance, Sergeant, with the countersign."

He advanced and whispered the correct word to me.

"Advance, rounds," I stated, and stood at shoulder arms until they passed. Grand rounds were the

Army's way of making certain that their sentinels were awake and on the lookout.

Once they passed, I returned to my trite duty. However, just as in Memphis, I was disturbed by sounds coming out of the dark. And, just like in Memphis, they were not made by animals. But before I could know that, I picked up my lantern and patrolled in that direction. Stepping softly and slowly, I came upon a light shining in the distance. I extinguished mine and gradually crept toward the small glow.

I was about sixty to seventy yards from my post and knew I should have called out for my commanding officer, but something told me to examine the situation for myself first. After all, I felt I was quite competent in my abilities to attend to the circumstance. The closer I came, the more I understood the noise as voices.

Still, I approached cautiously. When I got near enough, I knelt down behind some thick bushes and low-standing trees. What I observed was treasonous. Two Confederate soldiers on horseback held a gun to three negro slaves, a woman and two men. Another Rebel drove a wagon harnessed to one horse and waited for the outcome.

"We trailed you niggers clear from the Maynard plantation," one of the horsemen said as he got down from his steed. He pulled chains from the saddlebag and began restraining one of the slave's ankles, connecting it to the other ankle.

The female of the runaway trio stepped forward and spoke. "You has to let us go. We 'mancipated, sir."

With a quick and stunning blow, the Rebel soldier backhanded her hard across her cheek. "Shut up, ya whore. Ain't no 'mancipation for you. You and these other niggers are going straight back to the cotton field."

She held her cheek from the sting of his hand and watched as he began putting the shackles around the same man's wrists. "You's was 'posed to help us. You's a Yankee." She pleaded with another man, who stepped from the shadows. My jaw dropped agape with surprise when the sky-blue uniform trousers came to light in the shine of the moon. It was none other than Albert Turner, the same man I had tussled with in Memphis on our way into town.

"I ain't fightin' this war for no darkies, you colored bitch. You'll do well if you find some respect for your white master," he declared as he walked toward her, and added a slap to her face of his own.

The slave man who had not yet been shackled plunged forth at Albert but was quickly inhibited by the other Rebel soldier. They all had a good laugh before fettering chains to him as well.

I knew I needed to do something, but there were four of them in total. My rifle against their four didn't seem enough, and I also noticed pistols strapped to their waists, but I had sworn an oath to myself to lay my life on the line for the principle of freedom, and here were flesh-and-blood manifestations of what that oath was meant to protect. I had to try something, and fast.

They were beginning to load the fugitives into the wagon when I sprang into action, propelling myself toward them in an attempt at surprise. I held my arms steady, my eye behind the barrel, focused on each of them. "One move from any of you and I will blow your goddamned head off!" My voice was firm yet beseeching, and I threatened once more. "Not one move, Johnny."

I averted my attention to Albert. "This is how you serve the Army? This is how you serve your country?"

"This country has it all wrong, wanting to make a colored equal to a white man. What sense is there in that, in giving them freedom? They're too stupid, too ignorant to know how to take care of themselves. It'll be worse for them in the end. They're animals, and should be treated as such." His voice was filled with venom for a race he knew nothing about.

"Those black folks are coming with me," I ordered.

In that instance, one of the Confederates stepped forward. I saw him out of the corner of my eye, and immediately centered my focus and rifle directly at him. He stilled at once in his tracks, as I repeated my threat again. "I swear on my father's dead body, I will kill you."

Where this particular bravery had emanated from, I wasn't quite sure. Although my stance and attitude portrayed confidence, my insides were shaking uncontrollably over the outcome of this unfortunate night of guard duty.

"Turn them over," I directed the Rebel soldier, who had just loaded them in for the ride back to their owners.

"Not a chance," he responded, spitting out snuff as he did, his face callous with loathing.

"I would do as I say, because if I call on an officer, he and the whole of the guard will rally forth to the disturbance."

"Tell you what." Albert walked over to the closest slave sitting on the edge of the wagon, and continued. "I'll give you one."

"You'll give me all." I inched forward slightly, my finger steady on the trigger.

"Come now, one is enough. I'll give you the darkie wench."

They all chortled again at this, and with just that small distraction he leaped at me, grabbing for my gun. I had scuffled with him before, but a black curtain of hate fell over his graveyard eyes as we clashed and struggled for the weapon. At the end of our scramble, he retrieved my arms.

Perspiration filmed over my skin while my heart pained me with its racing beat, fearing for my life at the hands of a comrade. He held the barrel to my temple and cocked the trigger. I closed my eyes.

"You willin' to die for a darkie?"

"I'm willing to die for civility and humanity." My body trembled and quivered, for I knew I was about to meet my maker. I braced myself for death, when out of nowhere, a man appeared behind him and placed the end of a Remington revolver to the back of Albert's head.

As this occurred, the three Rebels drew up their weapons and aimed at us three, while I grabbed back my own rifle and took aim at them. It was a circle of guns drawn on each man, and no one willing to shoot first. I snapped my head toward the kind stranger who just saved my life, only to see Bradley standing there, fearless. My comrade, my best friend, had come to my rescue from out of thin air. Incredible to say the least, and yet, still not out of imminent danger.

He smirked at me, but only a bit, so as to calm but not make light of the situation all the same. No one would discharge their arms. The shooting of any weapon in this bizarre standoff would draw unwanted attention to any and all. Everyone sought to escape with their lives intact, but that was yet to be determined.

"All right then," Bradley said. "This is what's going to happen, gentlemen." He spoke precisely at the enemy soldiers. "You're going to turn over the contraband to us and be on your way, or you'll be hanged by the United States Army. The choice is yours." The air was thick with tension as each man looked from one to the other, debating their options.

After a few moments of thought, they swiftly tossed the woman from the wagon to the ground, followed by the other two fugitives. They unlocked the stiff and hard shackles from their hands and feet, and got back up on their horses. "This ain't over, Billy Yank. General Pemberton's waitin' for y'all in Vicksburg. He knows you're comin'." With that, they rode through the woods, back into the blackness of night.

When I turned my focal point back to Albert, Bradley still had his pistol pointed at the back of his head. "What are you going to do with me?" he asked apprehensively.

"What makes you think I shouldn't just murder you in cold blood, you treasonous bastard?"

"Just let me go with them." He nodded to the wagon, implying he should side with the Rebels. "I ain't dyin' for no filthy darkie."

Without hesitation, we led him and the newly freed slaves back to camp. He was under the arrest of the Army, and would suffer the consequences of being a traitor to his country. The officers listened to our account of the details, and by morning it was decided he would be executed by a firing squad. There was no time to waste in situations like this. Justice had to be swift, as Vicksburg was calling and our march could not be detained.

At sunrise, a firing squad of six sharpshooters was assembled. They were each handed a rifle that was not their own. Only half the guns held ammunition, so that no one soldier felt as though he was the one to take the lethal shot. It was said the men were more likely to aim to kill if they were not entirely blamed for it.

They attempted to blindfold Albert but he refused, insisting that he would die like a man, looking into the eyes of his killers. He was then tied to a tree so he couldn't move. The firing squad stood only about thirty paces from their human target. The officer observed his squad and began his orders. "Ready..." The men came to arms. "Aim..." They lifted their arms and aimed at Albert's heart. He then directed his words to the treasonous criminal. "Do you know why you are about to die?"

"Yeah, because I don't love darkies," he answered.

"May God have mercy on your soul." But the officer's prayer was soon interrupted.

To my shock, Albert whipped his head toward me, a mere spectator of the event, and started to yell. "I know your secret, Melvin! I know you're a—"

"Fire!" came the last command before he could get the words out.

In a rapid series of loud pops, six shots went off almost simultaneously. Albert's body jerked in place, his head falling forward with his body. He slid down the tree as far as the rope around his waist would allow, and came to a stop hunched and hanging over his crossed legs. Blood stained and marked the tree of his demise.

Disbelief swept over me, and I found myself looking to the sky, praising the Lord for his swift hand of wrath. While the Army physician checked his neck for a pulse, Bradley peered over at me. "What did he mean by secret? Are you keeping something from me?"

His concern was apparent, but I put an end to that concern by simply saying, "I've no secrets, friend. You're like a brother to me."

Grateful for the continuance and life of my secret, I helped to dig the shallow grave in which we would bury Albert. The men spat on the small mound of dirt as they passed, the most respect he would see from his former fellow soldiers as they went back to packing up their gear for our march southward to Vicksburg.

Chapter Fourteen

Just before we pushed forward into Louisiana, the last leg of our journey, Bradley and I were handed a promotion to sergeant. Another stripe to the two already there. The promotion came after the incident with Albert, the Confederates, and the fugitive slaves. We bivouacked the night of April 28, and while Ted slept I sewed the stripes onto my and Bradley's uniforms. Bradley was unaware of my gesture, as I temporarily stole his frock while he slumbered, but we had to march so quickly there was no time to properly thank him for saving my life. I contemplated my situation as I sewed.

I had been almost found out several times now, and each time it built my anxiety higher and higher. Twas not fun to feel so insecure. Remaining poised was becoming more difficult, but I was compelled. I had to remain steady and sanguine, for time and circumstance had made my heart fond of the cause of the Union. I was in this with my brothers, to whom I had become so close. As close as I could, that is, knowing what I knew about myself. I was a soldier. I was a comrade. In the eyes of an oppressed slave, I was a hero fighting for their freedom from the shackles and chains of bondage. And stick it out with this thorn in my side, I would.

That morning, there was much elation and energy among the men. We brewed our coffee, ate our breakfast, packed our haversacks, and marched the rest of the Louisiana levee to the Mississippi River. There, boats awaited to transport us across the river and into Mississippi. We landed in Bruinsburg and immediately got to marching twelve more miles down dusty roads and hilly countryside. The boys were much more pleased by the fragrant aroma of Mississippi flowers than they were the alligators of Louisiana.

We arrived near Port Gibson by dark, and were told of General McClernand's advanced corps defeating the enemy, who marched out of Vicksburg to meet our Army. Our beloved General McPherson held confidence in us enough that we trailed the enemy, hearing cannonading in the distance. We wanted a part in it. We got close enough to the retreating Army that we skirmished with them up ahead. My company had no role in it, though. Midnight approached, and we hunkered down in a ravine for the rest of the night.

❧❧❧❧

The sun peeped through the tall trees, shining its delightful rays upon my face. The morning was calm and pleasant, as a variety of birds warbled and sang as if all were peace and quiet. On our march that morning, we came upon several houses that had been abandoned by civilians wanting to flee the approaching Union Army. Down there, they built the chimneys on the outside of the house, and they still stood, alone, even when the house had been burnt. This had been the case with several homesteads we passed. One of our boys chased a chicken clear around one of these houses, determined to make a meal of it. We collected two days' rations at a time, but foraged off the countryside as necessary. Picking vegetables on our way to Rocky Springs was a real treat since they were nonexistent in our rations.

When word came through the line that we were close to the rear of the enemy's retreating lines, we double-quicked, hot on their heels. By evening, we caught sight of them crossing Hankinson's Ferry on the Black River. We swiftly charged upon them and fired, while our artillery shelled them. Some of them were shot trying to cross that bridge, yet none of us knew which of our bullets had hit them. It was but a small taste of what was to come. They retreated farther down the same road that led to Vicksburg. We camped for the evening.

Thinking the Rebels had retreated completely and with the sun still on its descent, some of the boys couldn't refuse the temptation of having a swim in the river. How unfortunate for them when their complaint was no longer of the cold water, but of being shot at repeatedly from Rebels that filled the surrounding woods. They ran for their lives, some not bothering to collect their clothes, instead running for camp as bare as an infant. The enemy's rear guard did not leave easily, but our canister shot was hot enough for them to finally retreat with the rest of their Army.

While guarding Hankinson's Ferry, we realized its importance, as it was a clear and open route for our supply wagons. It was imperative that the route stay open and free of the Confederate Army. Mail arrived to camp that day, and the men were jubilant. Nothing was as exciting to a soldier as receiving letters from home. Sadie had written me twice since leaving Memphis, but this time I received a letter from Uncle Lester.

Dear Melody, it began, and I cursed him for using my birth name after having told him of my new identity. I curled my body around the folded paper, attempting to shield it from the wandering eyes of others, and began reading my uncle's words.

> *Dear Melody,*
>
> *I do hope this letter finds you in good health and spirits. I take up this pen to write you a few lines. It is with great pleasure to inform you I have sold your father's farm, and am inclined to hold the proceeds until your destined and safe return. Do write me with detailed instructions on your wishes.*
>
> *I am not at all in agreement with your decision to join and remain in the Army, and I do wish you would consider coming home. Come home, Melody, and find a good man to share in your life and your burdens. The military is no place for a woman. Come to your senses at once before you humiliate yourself, or worse yet, become jailed, or even killed. War is for men. I will not consider the ways in which your father reared you, for you know better.*
>
> *Very respectfully,*
> *Uncle Lester*

The only information I retained from his correspondence was that he sold the farm. If I could make it through this war, I may be compelled to begin a life somewhere away from Borden, away from Indiana, and make a new life for myself as a man. I would let

Sadie choose a property and I would purchase it. We could live happily together, perhaps as man and wife. Oh, the joy I felt in such a dream. A dream I was soon shook from as we were about to march again.

⚜⚜⚜

Leaving Hankinson's Ferry, we camped and passed through Rocky Springs, where we found fresh, cold spring water straight from the breast of the hills. Delicious water indeed. We filled our canteens and continued our march toward Utica. Quite frankly, none of us knew exactly what General Grant's intentions were. Some said we were going to surround Vicksburg, and others insisted we were searching for the Rebel's weakest point, so as to strike him a heavy blow there. Which way we took Vicksburg mattered not, for when General Grant gave the forward order, we unquestionably obeyed. He had never known defeat, and though I understood he wasn't the most sociable of men, he cared deeply for his soldiers. His soldiers, in return, gave him the utmost and deserving respect possible.

As we passed through, we came upon some civilian men of the area. They were surprised by the mass of Union troops passing through. "There must be at least a million of you'ns down here," one of them mused aloud.

"This ain't nearly half of our Army," Ted said, taunting on our way past.

They seemed like good Union-loving men, but we knew not to trust their words. Their sentiment, we knew, lay with the South. None had the courage to avow that loyalty to us, though, and we continued on to

Utica, watching our backs for Southern sympathizers. After all, they owned guns, too.

⚜ ⚜ ⚜ ⚜

After bivouacking for the night, we were ordered to draw two days' rations, pack up, and be prepared to move on a moment's notice. We received hardtack, coffee, bacon, salt, and sugar. I took great care in packing the hardtack into my haversack, for if a corner of it stuck out too far, it would stick me in my side, leaving a mark and making me uncomfortable. Once my canteen was filled, I tied my tin cup to it and proceeded into the line of march. Each step I took, the tin cup rattled as if I were a cow coming home from pasture. Our grand Army marched in solid columns with our regimental flag flying and waving in the spring breeze. Our brogans stepped in time to the drum and fife of the regimental band playing "Yankee Doodle" and "The Girl I Left Behind."

We stopped about three miles from Utica and set up camp. Bradley and I went to a house nearby in search of cornbread, but wandered upon the wrong one. When we got there, what we found was a young mistress, crying and alone. Her negro servants had up and left her upon hearing of President Lincoln's Emancipation Proclamation. The pitiful soul had not one clue as to how to cook, much less tend to housework. Her provisions were scant, and though we empathized with her dire situation, we were on the hunt for some of our own.

Her husband was a Confederate officer, and he promised her she would never see the likes of a Yankee soldier down here. We were likened to inform her that we were, in fact, down here.

"Y'all are nice-looking fellows," she said with surprise in her tone as she continued. "You're not at all the beasts I was told the Lincoln soldier is."

"We are as much human as you are, my dear." Bradley was polite if nothing else. We didn't overstay our welcome, and seeing we were still in search of something other than hardtack, we bid her good luck and went on our way.

We were able to steal some vegetables from the garden of another house, and when the mistress of that plantation ran after us, swatting a broom in our direction, her house negroes met us up the driveway and gave us a basket filled with apples and peaches. Just as we got back to the road, an old negress, easily in her seventies, called to us. When we approached her, she handed us fresh cornbread wrapped in a cloth napkin, and a jar of blackberry jam. Her eyes revealed much pain and suffering in her life. Her hardships were evident in the deep wrinkles that lined her face. "God bless the Yankee soldier," she simply said, and turned to go back to the house.

By the time we returned back to camp, we had just about made ourselves sick on cornbread and jam. "Strange how we have yet to come across a schoolhouse, isn't it?" Bradley asked, as we lay on the ground 'neath the shade of a tree.

"Indeed." I agreed, acknowledging the truth in his words. "In my opinion, the negroes and the lower-class whites of the area are more equal than the whites would like to admit. In all honesty, I can hardly determine what they are saying when they speak, be it white or colored."

After much debating between the two of us, our

full bellies could not permit consciousness any longer, and we both fell asleep. We awoke long enough to make our way back to our own tents. No sooner did we shut our eyes than we were woken again, and told to pack up and head out.

The stars were still covering the morning sky when we proceeded with our march toward the town of Raymond. Rumors abounded that we would meet our first battle upon arrival. Our band of brothers had become more than just comrades on this long and treacherous march. We had become family, each willing to lay down his life for the other. But as we approached Raymond, the voices of the boys so intent on a fight dissipated and ceased. I, too, was afraid of battle, but take up my musket, I would.

꧁꧂

At nine o'clock in the morning on the twelfth day of May, some skirmishing began in our front. By eleven o'clock, we were joined by two other regiments as we filed into a field to the right of the road. Within moments, firing commenced in our front, and the order came. "Attention! Fall in! Take arms! Forward! Double-quick, march!"

We moved swiftly, as did the Confederate bullets. In advancing about one hundred yards, we came upon a creek of which the bank was high. Without hesitation, we slid down it, and waded through knee-deep water. Once on the other side, we began firing at will. We were determined to whip the enemy here and now, so as to continue our march to the capital city of Mississippi, Jackson.

There was barely any cover for my company of

men, and our foe was in front of us with a wide-open space. Attempting to retreat back up the bank from which we had just descended was sure death. However, retreat was the furthest thought from our minds. The regiment to our right was giving way and wavering, until our valiant and beloved General Buckley rode up and down the line, corralling and forcing them back into the gap they had just created. His enthusiasm was contagious, and the boys fought courageously.

My heart pounded wildly with panic and fear. It took a number of moments for my hands to steady enough to make a difference in unloading my arms. I was so focused on firing and reloading that I only noticed my head and face were soaked in perspiration when it trickled into my eyes, burning as it did. In an effort to remain fixed on the enemy, I wiped the sweat with my sleeve. All the while, bullets whizzed and buzzed past my head. Along with musketry fire were the shells that burst forth from the cannons, shattering trees and causing a rainfall of twigs, leaves, and even whole, thick branches around us.

A fresh regiment of Confederates arrived to the field, screaming their Rebel yell as they charged us. Gripped with terror, I looked around me, searching the faces of my fellow green comrades, wondering if they were as scared as me. When I peered next to me, there knelt a young soldier with his rifle in his hands. His knuckles had turned white from the intense grip he had on it, almost as pale and ashen as his face was. His eyes were the size of saucers, and he was completely incapable of blinking. He was utterly paralyzed with fright. I felt as if I were the bravest soldier in our unit when I glanced down at his trousers and realized he had wet himself.

"Private!" I touched his shoulder in an effort to draw him back into the present. He flinched at the contact, his distress making him involuntarily jump with jitters. I continued. "You will be all right, but you must pull the trigger. Your brothers are counting on you."

His blank stare slowly returned to a more natural state as he fixated on my voice and eyes. With only a nod of affirmation, he began firing and reloading. I took my own despair, and using his as well, refocused my attention on the enemy in my front. Firing repeatedly, I could not tell you if any of my bullets connected. Even as a Rebel fell to the ground, who knew if that shot had come from my musket or someone else's.

The contest raged on for two hours at a furious pace. As men dropped to their deaths all around me, I watched the creek we fought in and near turn red with the blood that had been spilled for our country. Looking over to my right to check on the young boy that was frozen in terror, I witnessed a Minié ball crash through his brain. He fell over, killed instantly. My bottom lip trembled, the reality of war forcing itself upon me. This was glory? No, this was hell. All around me was the repugnant scent of death, and despair would strangle my heart if not for the fight in front of me.

As the battle rampaged on and the fighting became fiercer, we came so close to the enemy that hand-to-hand combat became inevitable. Men beat each other with the butts of their rifles and charged one another with bayonets. The pointed, sharp steel of the bayonets glistened and sparkled in the late morning sun as they impaled soldiers of both blue and gray.

Ghastly was the sight of bodies strewn in heaps

upon the ground. In all of the mayhem, my attention turned to Bradley, my lifesaver and friend. He was tangled up with a butternut Confederate, whose tan clothing was worn and torn. His feet were bare of shoes. He had Bradley's head in a lock under the crook of his arm, and he squeezed his neck tightly. Bradley's face turned deep red, and the veins in his head protruded from lack of circulation. He was struggling to breathe. I darted across the field and tackled the butternut to the ground, giving Bradley a chance to regroup and catch his breath.

Leaving the man I'd just set on his back, I turned to look for Bradley. The blood drained from my face as I watched, in unmitigated abhorrence, another Rebel soldier shove his bayonet into Bradley's chest, piercing his heart. The gray-backed soldier then withdrew his dirk, Bradley's blood dripping from it as he did. He had mortally wounded my best friend, and he appeared proud to have done so.

Witnessing Bradley writhe in pain on the ground awoke a part of me better left untested. My nostrils flared, and I bared my teeth like a rabid dog when I jerked my sight from the blood on his bayonet to his dirty, filthy face. Our eyes met, and the barbaric savage hidden deep within myself reared its ugly head. I lunged forward, raising my musket from its barrel, and swung it like a club, connecting with the side of his head, hard. The sound of his cracking skull was loud as I crushed the rest of his head. It was kill or be killed, and kill him I did.

Bradley lay on the ground, holding his impaled breast while blood poured from his wound over and between his fingers. Placing both hands underneath his arms, I dragged him out of the fray of martial killers. I knelt by his side and cradled him in my arms. It was difficult to watch him, to watch the life leaving his body. "You're going to be all right," I wished out loud.

"No, Melvin, I'm not." He struggled to speak, and brought his blood-covered hand from his chest to his eyes. He wiped his tears away, and added, "I am to meet my maker today."

"No, you're not," I said, panic-stricken as I attempted to stop the bleeding. His uniform was drenched in red, and even while my tears burned hot down my cheeks, my mind would not allow the thought of him dying. He couldn't die. I didn't think I could cope with yet another loss of someone I held so dear to my heart.

His breathing was labored and he found it hard to speak. "Melvin," he called out, his voice low and rattled. He grabbed the collar of my jacket and pulled me closer to his face. I held my ear near his mouth and listened with great intent. Concentration was a struggle as the battle raged on around us. His hand still grasping my collar, he brought the other hand to his coat and pulled from it the daguerreotype photograph we had taken together in Memphis. The tin image brought me back to that day and how proud we were to take the picture. "When the war is over, please take this photograph to my parents. Tell them I died for my country. Tell them I fought nobly and with honor."

"No! Bradley, you mustn't die. You can't." Tears burst forth, chasing each other down my cheeks and falling onto Bradley's face, which was covered in cartridge powder.

As I held his head in my hands, he began coughing up blood. He looked into my eyes with fear and trepidation, and softly said, "My dear Melvin."

They were his last words, as his hand fell from my coat to his side. His eyes remained open while he took his final breath. I glanced around, not focusing on any one thing. I was in a state of shock. I had just lost my closest friend, and in the same instance, killed someone for the very first time in my life. Taking another's life, even out of vengeance, was an awful, empty feeling.

I closed Bradley's gaping mouth and smoothed his eyelids down over his eyes. I cradled his dead body for a few moments more, unable to control the myriad emotions that overtook me as I sobbed for the loss of my comrade and friend.

Doing my best to compose myself in the midst of battle, I got up and finished dragging his lifeless body to the rear of our line. I backpedaled my feet, securing him under his arms as Minié balls whizzed past my head in their quest for death. The immense angst I held inside of me was pushed aside by disassociating myself from it and doing what was necessary. This was no easy task, as the balls cut through the air too high, snipped tree branches and leaves above, sending them falling around me.

While I kept watch of the surrounding areas, there were men of both blue and gray littering the field. I observed with horror soldiers wailing out their pain from their wounds. One Union soldier I passed as I lugged Bradley's body was missing half of his jaw. He ran around aimlessly, his hand holding what was left of his mouth. Each time he screamed in agony his tongue flailed about without a place to settle. Another soldier, this one in gray, attempted to crawl toward his comrades, minus a leg. Blood trailed his severed limb, and just before he reached the Rebel line, he came to a stop and never moved again.

When I finally laid Bradley's body down behind a thick tree, I returned to the melee. Men were falling from my company rapidly. I found the second lieutenant in command severely wounded, and the orderly sergeant dead. Thence, I found myself in charge of the handful remaining. Hand-to-hand combat came to a close as Union reinforcements came up from our rear. With their help, we routed the enemy back down Raymond road, through the town of Raymond, and prepared for battle in the state capital of Jackson.

Before we set up camp in Raymond, I and a couple of my fellow comrades dug a hole deep enough to lay Bradley's body to rest. Four of us lifted him and set him in his final place of eternal slumber. As tears spilled down my face, I gathered dirt on my spade and buried my friend. Each pile of soil thrown onto his rigor-mortised body was a reminder of the reality and cruelty of war. We patted the mound of dirt and erected a cross made of two fairly large sticks we tied together. When his grave was complete, we removed our caps and bowed our heads in a moment of silence. I prayed for Bradley's soul, and hoped the Lord welcomed him through the gates of Heaven.

We left him there under the shade of that tree, and although we were sad upon the death of so many of our brothers, our will to fight was that much stronger to avenge them. When we set up our bivouac, we heard that the scuffle we had been in would be called the Battle of Raymond. *Raymond.* The name would be forever etched in my memory, and no doubt cause me much pain at the mere mention for the rest of my days. I was numb. And as I moved through camp—to where, I had no idea—I grabbed the whiskey bottle right out of a private's hand and took several huge gulps. Bradley was right when he said I would drink again. However, I didn't take a drink from only the stress of battle, but for the death of my beloved comrade.

Chapter Fifteen

Chatter around the camp was of every individual man's experience in his first battle. It was a sobering event to watch your entire life flash before your very eyes. The ultimate fear of death will cause a man to make resolutions if his life was spared, only to have those same resolutions fade as he walked from the battlefield victorious with his life. Negotiations never work with God. I know, for then my father would still be alive and I would still have known the sweet taste of Violet's beautiful lips. Negotiations ceased after being smited in the worst possible ways of the heart. If I could have traded places with my dear friend Bradley, I gladly would have. He could have known a life that included marriage and children, a life worth living with a legacy to leave behind. What had I to leave behind? A mound of dust made from the bones of an imposter, a fraud, a sick individual who could neither accept nor tolerate her role as a woman. I would rather be dead. However, God must have had a different plan for me, for I was still there. Through a haze of bullets and hatred from the enemy, I had survived. I had survived to fight another day, and only God knew why.

❧❧❧❧

On our way through Clinton the next day, we

were ordered to tear up the railroad that connected Jackson to Vicksburg. The Confederates would see no more supplies being run down this line. We would strangle the very life from not only the Rebel Army, but the civilians of Vicksburg as well. Whoever remained in the town would suffer the most despairing atrocities they had ever known.

I woke up that morning to a pouring rain. Our tent barely held the water out, as there were small holes and some wear from being repeatedly used as our residence. "Ted, wake up," I said, stirring him from sleep. "It's time to march again." My voice was thick with grief, and the doldrums took up the most space in my heart. There was no time to grieve, though. We had to march, so march we would.

My first step out of our tent ended in a splash of mud. The rain beat down on me, and I lifted my face to the open morning sky and allowed it to absolve me of my sins, of my grief, and of my guilt. I swallowed my despair in my throat and joined the rest of my men in preparing for march.

Our corps of soldiers started on its way. However, as we approached Jackson, the rain hardened, pelting the ground so forcefully it left deep puddles of dark, thick mud. Wading through it became difficult. Ankle-deep in muck, many of the men helped push the supply wagons and cannon caissons through low ruts. Officers' and their aides' horses plodded through puddles, splashing filthy water onto all as they passed. We were all soaked right down to our skin, but we toiled on for love of our country.

We received news that General Sherman had slid around to the right and captured the place. We were just a few miles away from Jackson, and when the word went down the line, we were so inspired that we ran without stopping to join the fight. Sherman's Army was to the right and McPherson's Army, that of our own, was in the immediate front. We routed the remaining Rebels, pushing the enemy through and past Jackson. They didn't stop their retreat until they were safe within the confines of Vicksburg and the Rebel line. On this night, our mud-soaked soldiers hoisted the Stars and Stripes proudly over the state capital of Mississippi.

For the next few days, we fought the persistent enemy all the way through Champion Hill, losing men not only to enemy fire but to disease as well. Typhoid and other illnesses spread rampantly through our ranks. But the thinner our ranks were made, the closer the ones left standing became.

It was incredible how we got to know each other better through the death and dying of battle. As we pushed our way through Champion Hill, we captured artillery, supplies, and Rebel soldiers. The men that could move and walk were taken to the rear, and quite happy to eat our Yankee provisions no matter how scarce they were. Apparently, they had absolutely no provisions to sustain their Army. These men were feculent and starved. Their tattered clothes barely qualified as uniforms. Most were barefoot.

Soldiers tended to grow closer as they realized the horrific ravages of war. The bodies dressed in gray littered our way, some dead, some wounded, both mortally and otherwise. The sounds of agony echoed through the moans of the dying. I came across one brave Confederate soldier, no more than fifteen years old. He lay on his back with a Minié ball lodged in his spine. He could move nothing but his mouth.

Tortured and pained, he begged me. "Would you be kind enough to share a swig of water, my brother?"

No words were needed in response. I knelt by his side, lifted his head, and gently poured some water into his mouth. He licked and lapped at it, his lips crusty and dry. "Damn this war," were his last words. His head fell to the side, and while I watched his life leave his worldly vessel, I remembered that he was someone's son. I pictured his mother receiving the heartbreaking news of his demise. I prayed they would tell her he fought valiantly for what he thought was right. He died fighting for his cause. I could not help but pity him, and hope that when this war was over, we may once more be brothers, sharing in peace under the same flag.

We ran over their works pell-mell as our Army advanced on at Big Black River. Routing the foe, we captured 2,500 prisoners and twenty-nine cannons. They had many rifle pits, but they were all on low ground, and when the word was given the Yanks hurried over them without much difficulty. We had no idea if the Rebels were drawing us into a trap, but we had no doubt we would be victorious, for when Grant said go we went, and felt safe in doing so. Every day brought with it new scenes fraught with dangers, hairbreadth escapes, and death, after which the ranks closed up the gaps and continued on, undaunted.

We camped within a few miles of Black River. That night, our Army made pontoons on which we crossed the river the next morning. McClernand was on the left, McPherson in the center, and Sherman to the right. It was in these positions the three grand corps would move to Vicksburg by different roads.

As we crossed the river and marched up the

bank, a brass band stood playing national melodies. We were so proud marching through the Rebel works. It was a magnificent sight to watch the long lines of infantry making their way over the pontoons. With flags flying in the breeze, we wound our way up the bluffs. The morning sun gleamed off the rifles that rested on our shoulders. Many cheers were heard from thousands who had already crossed and stood waiting on the bluffs above. This was to be our last stop before we knocked on the door of the hailed *Gibraltar of the West.*

❧❧❧❧

When we came to bivouac in a spot for the night, we did so without supper and no prospect of breakfast. Our rations had been entirely exhausted, and the boys swore and complained loudly. When General Frommer strolled through camp with his usual arrogant attitude, the boys put on a different face.

"You boys had supper yet?" he asked.

"No, General, we've had none," was the resounding group response.

"Well, boys, I've had none either. We'll have to fight for our breakfast."

"General, if you can stand it, I guess we can, too." We were tired, and we were hungry, but we were patriot soldiers, and we could and would withstand.

The bend in the Mississippi River allowed for natural fortifications of the city of Vicksburg that stood high on the bluffs of that bend. It also became surrounded, as our gunboats on the river awaited our arrival around the city by land. By May nineteenth, the three corps took their positions. General Sherman's Fifteenth Corps occupied the right of the line, resting on the river above. General McClernand's Thirteenth touched the river below, while General McPherson's Seventeenth—my corps—stood in the center. It took us nineteen days to march around Vicksburg.

The only fortification the Rebels still held was Fort Hill, a long line of earthworks outlining the zigzag courses of the hills. Their black field guns menaced from their portholes, bristling with defiance at us, the invaders.

❧❧❧❧

When I awoke that morning, I started by offering my thanks to God for sparing my pathetic life thus far. I was also presented another promotion, this one to Second Lieutenant. I was nearing the top tiers of my company, trading in my stripes for shoulder straps. The pride of my life was climbing the ranks of the Army. So proud was I that I sewed the straps to my filthy uniform jacket. None of us had bathed or had a change of fresh clothes in over a month, though we understood new suits were on their way. I wished they would come, for I could not fathom entering Vicksburg in such a disgraceful state. We would be more than ashamed for the ladies there to witness us like this. We were a strong fighting force, and we should look as such.

The city was within our sight, and the Confederate flag flew above the courthouse in plain view. Oh, what grandeur it would be to hoist the Stars and Stripes in its stead! All around the city, the hills were quite perpendicular and desolate, which provided us sustainable shelter from enemy batteries.

The rifle pits we occupied were close to the Rebel rifle pits opposite us, and it became a daring game to raise a head above their works, or ours. A hundred shots, or more, were directed at any poor soul brave enough to do so.

The weather was quite hot in the South. The air was thick and heavy, and the sun beating down on us made it difficult to breathe. The air was cooler at night when we did most of our work. One cool night, we opened a number of new pits and placed gabions on them. Gabions resembled round baskets filled with dirt. We were determined to breach their fort. Their fortifications were made by cutting away the back half of a hill, leaving natural obstructions facing us. They were supplied with large guns. However, they could not be used on us, as our rifle pits were on higher ground.

At three o'clock that morning, mortar shells were fired from our gunboats on the river, directed at the city. Every one of our cannons belched shot at the Rebels. Only the thundering of guns could be heard from miles away. Over a hundred cannons wreaked havoc on Vicksburg, shooting off everything from shrapnel and canister to grape and solid shot. Withstanding a hailstorm of such magnitude seemed impossible. It was, indeed, an awfully grand and dreadful spectacle.

A battle was about to take place, and the atmosphere among us was filled with much energy and a consuming fear. Quickly, the boys divested themselves of watches, rings, and other keepsakes. They placed them in the care of the cooks, who were not expected to see action. I wished to never see such a scene again. Fresh, painful memories of Bradley arose while I watched and listened to the men as they relieved themselves of trinkets that meant something to them. "If I never return, please give this ring to my father," said one brave soldier. Another, "Tell my wife and children I fought gallantly and faced the enemy head-on." Others hurriedly wrote their name on a small piece of paper and pinned it to their uniform, so they could be identified if killed in battle.

The order was given, and we moved up into rifle pits that were just a hundred yards from Fort Hill. We could hardly see anything as thick cannon smoke filled the air. Only the flash of guns and bursting of shells revealed the line to my right and left. About eleven o'clock, we received the signal to charge the enemy's works.

The lead was taken by the Seventh Missouri as they placed ladders against the fort and climbed to the top. All who scaled the ladder to the top were met with cold steel. Finding it impossible to penetrate the fort this way, we were commanded to retreat. I was relieved that my company didn't receive the chance to climb that ladder of death.

General Grant was not ready to give up the assault and make a proper siege of the city. Instead, we were told to take shovels and picks, and begin digging at once. As the weather became stifling hot, I feared sickness. Being wounded in action or becoming ill worried me to no end. Either event would surely end my military career. I was stalwart that ending my military career would be on my own terms.

Every day we sent canister and Minié balls into the enemy lines while we continued to dig our way underneath the fort. The great expectation of Grant was to blow the entire thing up from the bottom by setting a mine below it.

On May 25 and just days before my twenty-first birthday, General Pemberton, the Rebel commander, sent up a flag of truce. A halt in hostilities was agreed upon. They were not surrendering; they only wanted a break in the fighting to bury their dead, the bodies of both sides having lain in the field for three days.

During this six-hour recess, both armies mingled together with much delight. Some played sports. Others played cards. Conversation abounded about the events that had transpired since we arrived in their area. Many of our gray-clad counterparts observed that we should have Vicksburg. It was a matter of time, as far as they could see. Their provisions were running low, as was their ammunition supply. We shared our rations with them, even though ours were low as well, but at least we knew food and supplies were on the way. They were much pleased. After trading newspapers and coffee, we all returned to our respective sides.

It was odd to say the least, that we should enjoy each other's company so. After having shot at one another with the intention to kill, the mutual feeling of hate was met with mutual inklings of fondness. Many of our ranks were brothers and other kin of blood, fighting for opposite sides of this war of secession. My heart broke to watch a Confederate soldier who was the father of another dressed in blue. I felt their pain as they embraced one another tightly. He was hugging his baby good-bye, knowing full well they may kill each other for what they believed in, come the next fight.

❧❧❧❧

It was the twenty-ninth day of May and my day of birth, a yearly reminder that my existence meant my mother's demise. We also received mail that day. It was very rare for me to receive communication from anyone, but this day, I received a letter from Sadie. A wonderful birthday gift! It was a brief correspondence, but enough to lift my spirits, which had been mired in the realistic abyss of war.

> *My dear Melvin,*
>
> *I do pray this letter finds you well and in good health. Memphis has not been the same since you departed. My life seems to get no better, and I find myself dreaming of seeing you again someday. You made a promise to me, which I do hope you will make good on when this awful war is over.*
>
> *May God watch over you, Melvin.*
> *Yours affectionately,*
> *Sadie*

I missed Sadie. I missed the affection of a woman. However, I reminded myself that my life was best lived alone, without a companion. My Army brethren would have to suffice in the way of companionship and family.

The most tantalizing part of her letter was the sweet smell of perfume she sprayed on the paper. En route from Memphis, down the river to Vicksburg, the scent had lost some of its punch. But the faint aroma wafted up my nose and through my senses. My body responded to it in ways I hadn't felt for some time. They were familiar still, and I quashed them with great difficulty until they disappeared altogether. The cannon took up belching shot at the city once more.

That night, I sat on top of a hill all by myself and watched mortar shells fly from the gunboats on the river. They were shot high into the air and fell like stars as they dropped and exploded among the houses, reverberating through the hills. I saw several shells in the air at once, their lit fuses visible through the smoke. The destruction in the city must have been devastating, for we bombed them repeatedly and consistently from daybreak until evening, and beyond sometimes.

The prisoners we took told us the inhabitants were now living in caves dug out of the side of the hills. God bless the women, children, and aged that resided there. They surely suffered the most. If this siege continued much longer, many deaths would come from more than mortar shells. Sickness would run rampant in this heat and without proper food. The Rebels tossed their shot and shell into our quarters as well. They had been stingy with their ammunition, and we knew they were running very low on it. I held hope that they were also running very low on stamina, for all our sakes.

❧❧❧❧

Every day brought with it the sounds of the guns. Seemed I knew of no other sound, for the birds had even taken flight. The chirping and singing of these lovely winged creatures was replaced with the whizzing sound of the Minié ball and the explosions of the cannons. This morning, the twelfth day of June, General Frommer sought me out for a haircut. He said nothing to me as he moved through camp in my direction. Rather, he simply sat on a bale of cotton. When I made no move to serve his voiceless request, he asked, "Are you going to stand there and gawk at me, or are you going to give me a delightful trim?"

"Quite frankly, sir, do you really believe this is the most opportune moment for me to groom your hair and mustache?" It was a rhetorical question, since bombs were bursting all around us. Granted, to a certain extent we had all become a bit immune to the shot, but these were hitting our camp directly and indirectly.

Just as he was about to speak, an explosive shell came soaring through the sky. It skidded its landing at the top of a small hill but did not detonate. We all watched intently as it rolled down the hill, still intact, and right into a tent. Thank God the occupants were not home. We observed in horror as it exploded, the smaller iron balls that had lain in wait inside the shell spraying out in every direction. Men dove for cover and shielded their heads. All but General Frommer, who sat in the same spot, still waiting for his haircut.

No more words were spoken. He lifted my scissors and held them in the air for me. I peeked about for other projectiles. Finding none, I sighed deeply and took the scissors. I thought the man not only arrogant, but thoroughly insane as well. Who in their right mind would have a haircut in the middle of a barrage of case and canister shot, letting loose its deadly shrapnel?

I began to cut his hair, desperately trying to bring my focus to my task. But, through the afternoon sky, a sky filled with blue, a canister shot tore and landed with such force so as to break the earth open.

Dirt spewed and sprayed in all directions, and when the smoke cleared, we noticed a crater. The size was enough to bury a horse. In the center of the gaping hole was the projectile, still unexploded.

"Must be dead," Private Ellis said.

"I wouldn't be so sure," I chimed in, never stopping my scissors motion.

A minute or two more passed, and the shot still lay there. Private Ellis, curiosity getting the best of him, cautiously inched his way toward it.

"Ellis, stay away from there," I ordered. The closer he got, the more distracted I became. He was about five feet away from it when I became alarmed enough to yell once more. "Private Ellis. Step away from that canister."

He ignored me and instead knelt beside it. In a state of panic, I threw the scissors down and frantically started for him. Upon further examination, he looked up in a hurry and said, "It's all good, Lieutenant. It's a failed shot. It's dead."

Boom! The cylindrical object burst and exploded, sending parts of Private Ellis in different directions. By the time I got to him, all that was left was his torso. His head had been severed in such a way that the skin hanging from his skull looked like ground up pork meat. It lay about twenty feet from his body. His limbs all tore off and lay scattered around the area. Blood filled the hole where the projectile had landed and where Private Ellis lost his life.

The hardtack I had just consumed came up and out of my mouth as I vomited over the gruesome sight. Men came running from everywhere to help, only to find the same severed body. They got to digging a shallow grave and buried his several remains. And through it all, I was still expected to finish General Frommer's shave. "You can't be serious, sir," I said, exasperated over his lack of emotion or respect for a young boy that had just lost his life, and in such a tragic manner.

"You can't save the world from stupidity, Cofield. Do you think it was smart to run toward a bomb that had not yet detonated?"

My eyebrows inverted toward one another, and I grimly replied, "Whether you think he was stupid or not, he was someone's son. A human being worth saving. What kind of man are you, General?"

Such insubordination could land me in some serious trouble, and he knew it. He looked up at me from where he sat, and his tone shifted. "I had a son once, too. He was smart and funny, and full of life." He paused, staring off into the distance as if remembering the events that were to come from his mouth next. "My son was seventeen years old and about to go to university when he contracted consumption. I watched my boy deteriorate right in front of my eyes. He died in my arms." Again, he looked up, and with a perpetual, agonizing pain, he continued. "You will have to forgive me for my resentfulness of watching a stupid boy, no more than my son's age, run without care or concern toward an object that he knew could kill him. My son wouldn't have been so careless and ignorant. But my son wasn't allowed to live to show you his wits. That young man just threw his life away. My son's life was taken." He choked on his last words, and added, "Now give me a proper shave."

I felt for him. I, too, knew what it was like to lose someone to disease. The hopelessness of not being able to make them better. The void that was left was there forever. The empty feeling never filled. I looked at him, really looked at him, for the first time. I saw the man and the father, not the emotionless General. "Well then," he said, prodding me on. I took the straight blade and finished his grooming session.

Once all was finished, he peered into the small mirror I provided. Seemingly satisfied, he got up, grabbed for his feathered hat, tipped it toward me, and placed it on his head. He walked away through scattered cannon fire, ending our interaction for the day. I didn't know if I had a better respect and understanding of him, or if I loathed him that much more.

Chapter Sixteen

The buildings of Vicksburg, I presumed, were riddled with holes from shot and shell. It would appear that not all of the women exited the city, instead choosing to brave it out. Their atonement and hardship were worthy of a better cause. Oh, how we would worship them had they been on our side. However, they were not, and their struggle might well continue for a time longer.

Several large siege guns were placed in the rear of our division. They were so heavy that it took ten yoke of oxen to haul them each into their positions. I observed as one of them spit a huge solid shot out into the sky. It was clearly visible during its flight across the hills toward the city. These guns were a nine-inch caliber, twelve feet long, and like the monster it was, its voice was a loud growl. How the city was surviving this deluge of shot and shell I had not the slightest idea. It seemed inconceivable to me.

Our line of rifle pits was so close to Fort Hill that one of the boys threw a piece of hardtack into their line. A Rebel satisfied our curiosity of its arrival by puncturing it with his bayonet and raising it in the air. During the din of musketry and cannonading, we noticed that some of the boys who had been wounded in Raymond were returning to rejoin the fight with us. I knew it was foolish to even think, but I couldn't help seeking them out, looking for Bradley. His smiling face appeared in my imagination, and before my emotions could get the best of me, I pushed the thoughts away. It was survival of the mind, trying to retain my sanity, and realizing that everyone I loved either died or abandoned me. It was enough to make sure I never let anyone get close to me again.

The enemy's guns were no match for us. Sherman's guns firing from the east, McClernand's guns firing from the west, McPherson's guns firing from the rear, and the mortars firing from the north—all surrounded and were aimed directly at the core of the city. It was a testament to the will and courage of our enemy that they should withstand such an assault on a daily basis. We were sure, though, that the eventual outcome would be victoriously in our favor.

That afternoon, General Grant rode through camp. The butt of a cigar was pursed between his lips as he rode his horse through a throng of soldiers, cheering and applauding him. His expression never changed. There was no smile upon his worn and rugged face. The war had taken a toll on him; that was obvious. The wrinkles on his forehead were deep, and only made him look sterner. The men respected him for his steady hand and patience during this siege. Some of the men yelled their enthusiasm as he strutted past them. "Give us the word, General and we will take Vicksburg!" Others pledged their complete loyalty. "We will follow you wherever you lead!"

He simply tipped his hat and continued through camp, inspecting his men as he did so. At the time I wondered how such a successful leader could be so ambivalent toward his men, choosing an aloof posture and remaining essentially solitary. I was soon to discover why such an attitude was attractive.

It seemed, after the battle of Raymond, that

Ted began distancing himself from me, the reasons for which I knew not still. His avoidance of me would normally bother me. However, after Bradley's tragic demise, I was satisfied with his deliberate apostasy. Coffee became my best friend instead. Whenever I could, I took my cove oyster can, filled it with water, and hung it from its bent wire bale over a fire. It took about five minutes to boil but was well worth the wait.

While I sat and enjoyed my freshly brewed cup, I pondered my role in our company of men. Being second in command brought me much pride and joy, without them knowing I had become the matriarch of our company. Though in feeling such pride and joy, I wondered if the men would still respect me if they knew I was a woman. Sadly, not one part of me felt they would. Perhaps keeping an emotional distance was healthy for a leader, not feeling that tug on the heart that inevitably would lead to heartbreak each time a soldier was wounded or killed in battle. Maybe this was why General Grant kept his distance from the men. He needed to keep that cool exterior. It was just too exhausting to keep putting the pieces of the heart back together after feeling such loss. I also chose not to get close to anyone. Such as it was, certain boys did strum my heartstrings with their stories of home and family, and the sickness that prevailed being away from them. Privately, I still longed for that kind of love.

Between the heat and the general filth of our bodies and uniforms, some of the boys had taken up boiling their pants. The tiny creatures that festered there were quite annoying when they bit flesh. It was understandable to take up such a practice, but it was also sheer entertainment to watch a soldier pull up a pair of boiled trousers. The boiling shrank them, and they became so short that they didn't even reach the tops of their brogans. The stench from dirty men, wounded and dying men, and the graves of the dead recently buried, all blended together to create a repugnant odor I found difficult to tolerate.

The men also got to playing a rather disgusting game with their head lice: placing wagers on whose lice would race off a plate first. Sergeant Wagner won more than his fair share of greenbacks, until they discovered he was heating his side of the plate before dropping in his competitors. His lice would hit the hot plate and practically jump right off. After all, a fire was set on his ass. When the gamblers found him out, it wasn't the plate that was heated any longer, it was the conversation. He was fortunate that he wasn't physically assaulted. The boys knew better. Punishment would ensue and no one wanted that.

∿∿∿∿

The morning of June 25, we learned that the tunneling we had dug for weeks had finally reached under Fort Hill. Filling our target with 2,200 pounds of gunpowder, we took up lines the rest of the day in preparation for the big event. We filled the trenches with men and were preparing for an all-out assault in an attempt to carry the fort.

While the trenches filled and roadways were created for artillery to pass over, the rest of the infantry took up positions in hollows and any other available places near the Rebel works where they could not be detected. Our regiment was marched some distance up a hollow, not far from Fort Hill.

At about 3:30 in the afternoon, the mine was detonated. The air filled with debris and the earth trembled. Men, timber, and dirt alike were tossed in every direction. My company was close enough to the explosion that our faces were sprayed with earth of all kinds. The explosion was the signal for the artillery around the line to let loose its rain of shot and shell on the Rebel works.

Our troops charged into the open crater left by the blast. The hole was about forty feet wide and approximately twelve feet deep. We watched in horror as our boys became easy targets for the recovering Confederates. They were pinned down, and the Rebels took advantage by pointing their artillery at the hole and firing with devastating results.

My company, led by myself and my immediate superior, Captain Elmer Peabody, found itself in the midst of this cannon fire. Many attempted to scale the wall of the crater only to find the Confederates had constructed a parapet across the back of the redans, blunting our assault.

What appeared to initially be our advantage quickly turned into theirs. They threw hand grenades at us, each exploding with great devastation. Those that clung to the wall of the pit fell to their deaths, or to the agonizing pain of dismemberment. Fear abounded and chaos ensued as officers attempted to scream and holler orders at men that were panic-stricken. They ran over each other in an effort to escape this hailstorm of lead.

Some courageous Rebels used a blanket to catch the grenades we tossed up at them, only to toss them back at us before they exploded. A few of our men tried their damndest to throw them above the crater wall, but failed at their own expense. The explosives rolled back at them, exploding and tearing their bodies to pieces. The blood of our nation spilled like a river inside that godforsaken crater.

Eventually, with the aid of our own artillery and sharpshooters, we reached the parapet. Some hand-to-hand combat took place, but ultimately the Rebels gave up the front of their fort. No sooner did we push them back than a Union work party began preparing gun emplacements, digging rifle pits to protect the section we had just gained.

I hurried back to the crater to survey the human damage. The results of the Rebel hand grenades and the short-fused shells they rolled down the walls were annihilating. A mound of mangled and broken men writhed in torment and anguish. The moans of the dying echoed out of the earthen cavity.

"Help!" I heard from many. But then I heard specifically, "Mel. Help me. Please!"

I searched the mess of men until my sight halted on Ted. He was clinging to the inside of the crater, clawing at the soil in an attempt to climb up and out. Confused by his lack of progress, I glanced down. His leg had been hit with shrapnel from an exploded shell. It was ripped open below the knee, and his shin bone was not only exposed, but had been broken and splintered in several places.

"Don't leave me here to die, Mel. Please." His face was wet from tears. He held his hands high, wanting me to pull him out.

"Wait," I shouted, and ran for help.

Returning with five men and a thick rope, I threw it down to him and said, "Tie it around your waist."

He did as he was told, and we all hoisted him up, farther, farther, until he was out of the hole. I held him in my arms as he cried like a babe. The pain his body was enduring caused much stress on him.

"How bad is it? I have yet to look," he asked, hoping for an answer he knew would not come. I took a gander at his wound and, without intention, turned my head and vomited. His mangled leg was badly broken, the flesh shredded, hanging off the bone.

He grabbed me by the collar of my jacket and pulled me to him. Tears cut through the dirt and sweat on his face as he interrogated me more. "Am I going to lose my leg?"

I didn't want to lie to him. However, the truth would crush his spirit. "Maybe the doctors should be the judge of that, yes?"

Our eyes connected and he searched my soul. He knew he would lose his leg, and saw I just didn't have the heart to break his.

"You're a good friend, Mel. I'm sorry for avoiding you as of late," he said, apologizing through his agony.

"We've no time for that, Ted. We need to get you some medical attention." He was bleeding at an alarmingly fast rate. Although I knew that he felt bad for putting distance between us and for the jealousy he felt for my successes, I admired and respected his apology as he faced the amputation of his right limb.

I was able to obtain an ambulance stretcher for him, but could not go with him to the field hospital. While they wrapped a tourniquet above his knee, I bid him farewell. "Godspeed, Ted."

For the next week, work parties of pioneers got to digging another tunnel under the rest of the fort. The Confederates were desperate to stop the tunneling underneath their lines, and frantically began digging and exploding counter-mines. All of their efforts failed, and on July 1 we set off a second explosion that ripped through the fort and parapet, leaving an even bigger crater than the last. Realizing our mistake from the previous explosion, we did not charge their works. The bloodbath from June 25 was still fresh in our minds.

We pushed the Rebels closer to the breaking point, and on July 3 word was sent down the line that the Confederates had asked for surrender terms. That afternoon, General Grant and General Pemberton met under the shade of a tree a short distance from the fort. Not long after, an exchange of terms was agreed to, and Pemberton surrendered Vicksburg.

As one company after another received word, cheers among more cheers could be heard in unison. "Hurrah!" and "Huzzah!" were shouted with glee. The smiles of the men were testament to the pride they held after enduring and suffering through forty-seven days of pure and utter hell. We all rejoiced that the news would speed its way north to loved ones who had prayed for us.

We had no doubt dealt a death blow to the Rebellion, or at least there in the west. Vicksburg had been the boast of the enemy, who thought it impregnable. They consistently defied the Army of the West to take it. Were it not for the untiring energy and skill of our gallant general, U.S. Grant, we would not know the sweet taste of victory. The Stars and Stripes would now float majestically over the besieged town. May history remember the brave souls that gave their lives for our great country. The courageous men who died at Raymond and Champion Hill shall not be forgotten. They did not die in vain.

Chapter Seventeen

The lovely sound of morning birds chirping replaced the horrid sounds of explosions that had become routine. It was a glorious day, for it was the fourth of July, and our country's day of independence. The boys gaily brewed their coffee as the sun made its ascent into a pink and orange sky. They ate their hardtack as if it were a roast beef supper. Not a grumble of a complaint could be heard from one soldier.

When breakfast was finished, we gathered joyously into lines of march. With our flags and drums and noisy cheering, we marched into the city we had fought so hard to possess and occupy. Spread-eagle speakers boasted their nationalistic pride as we all sang along to patriotic songs.

The deeper we marched into the town, the more fragrant the trees became. The sweet smell of magnolias drifted through the summer air. While troops set up camp on various estates, my company staked its place at the Livingston plantation. We were setting up our tents when General Frommer approached me.

"Lieutenant Coffield."

"Yes, sir," I responded.

"No need to pitch a tent. You'll be in the main house with me."

The befuddled look on my countenance compelled him to add, "I need a trim and a shave, and

I've decided you will be my new aide-de-camp. This also means you'll be expected to assist me in my duties, and to transport messages and orders to different areas of the town."

"But sir, one must be a first lieutenant to be an aide to a general."

"Well, so be it, Coffield! You are now a first lieutenant, and as your first duty as first lieutenant, you shall give me a trim and a shave." With a subtle nod, an indication to follow him, he hopped on his horse and led the way down the rest of the dirt drive. I practically ran after him trying to keep up. The road was a mile long to the mansion, and as we approached I was taken with awe at its majesty. The grass was a lush green, greener than I had ever seen back home in Indiana.

As we neared, the negroes greeted us with much enthusiasm, offering us cornbread and other things to eat. The wealthier plantations had been able to hide and stash some of their provisions, so this was a different scene than the one the Confederate Army suffered. General Frommer trotted through them and continued toward the house. I, on the other hand, collected as much of the delicious-smelling treats as I could handle. My belly begged to be fed something other than hardtack.

"The house occupants..." he started to say, but I didn't understand the rest, for the back of his head faced me.

I ran faster to catch up, dropping some of the edibles I had just gathered. "Sir, I didn't hear what you said." My voice shook as I ran.

"The occupants of this house were asked to leave, but have insisted on remaining," he said, keeping up his pace atop his horse. "Regardless, this will be our headquarters now."

The driveway curved around in a semi-circle, and we came to a stop in front of the pure white house. The structure was palatial with its large, round, white columns and extended veranda. The second level of the veranda included an intricately designed wrought iron railing. Three dormer windows protruded from the third. An ornate variety of roses and other lovely flowers surrounded the front.

He climbed down out of the saddle, and I followed him up the steps and through the front doors. We entered the foyer of the house, and I was suddenly thrown into a different world. A world I was not accustomed to. A world filled with bustle and activity. Servants busying themselves with cleaning, cooking, and catering to the wishes of the plantation mistress. My first few moments upon entering their abode were spent observing the bustling activity.

"Do what you need to do, but do stay out of the way of plantation business," the mistress said firmly to General Frommer. "My husband is an officer in the Confederate Army, and although you Yankees have taken control of Vicksburg, I would anticipate the same respect and dignity you would show your own mother."

While she chastised and instructed the General, I couldn't help but take a look around. The parlor was decorated with the most gilded and lavish adornments, from the long baroque drapes to the elegant double spoon-back sofas. The furnishings and carpet were undoubtedly of fine European quality. My eyes trailed the entirety of the room until they came upon the most beautiful woman I had ever seen in my life.

She sat in a chair surrounded by black children sitting on the floor around her. They listened intently as she read to them. I gazed at her thoroughly, without interrupting her lesson. Her delicate features were mesmerizing, and I found it difficult to take my eyes from her. High cheekbones were complimented by full, voluptuous lips. Her petite nose matched her tapered chin, and her skin was flawless. Her long, silky blond hair was tied up, with small ringlets of curls falling softly by her ears. However, the most captivating feature she possessed was her eyes. They were bluer than the skies above, twinkling bright as stars in the darkest of nights. If her eyes were the ocean deep, I would surely drown in them. They drew me in, and the closer I dared to peer into them, I swore I saw the sadness of heartbreak and the sorrow of pain. A common thread between us, and nay, not even knowing her name.

"May I help you?" she asked, breaking me from my spellbound trance.

Embarrassed, and without proper words, I replied, "No, ma'am." I tipped my hat and introduced myself. "My name is Melvin Coffield. Lieutenant Melvin Coffield."

"Well, Lieutenant, I am in the midst of a reading lesson, so unless the Yankee Army is forcibly removing us from our home, please do excuse yourself," she scathingly said.

"Yes, ma'am." Before excusing myself, I managed to ask, "Forgive me for asking, but what is your name?"

She looked up from the children to me, clearly agitated, but answered, "Becca. Rebecca Chamberlain."

"It's a pleasure to make your acquaintance."

Again, I tipped my hat.

Without a reply but with a disgusted look upon her face, she disregarded me and continued on with her lesson. She sent me away humiliated and completely, utterly, madly in love.

❧ ❧❧ ❧

General Frommer was quick to hand me a pair of scissors, and promptly found a seat. The sun shined its rays through the windows, giving me more than enough light to cut his hair. Unfortunately for him, it gave me enough light to see, without obstruction, into the parlor and Becca. Each time she peeked up toward me, I would avert my eyes. I didn't want to stare, but felt incapable of doing so. In one moment, she caught my gaze and our eyes connected for a brief instant. My stomach sank, and a feeling of lightheadedness consumed me. Never had I been so taken by a feeling of not only want, but need. My knees went weak, and, "God damn it, Coffield!" was what shook me back to the present. He pulled the mirror he held closer, patted his head, and berated me. "You nicked my scalp."

I certainly had. When I looked down, I noticed a whole patch of hair was gone, and a miniscule cut bled from his scalp. I apologized profusely, having destroyed my perfect record for neat haircuts. "I make you my aide and this is the gratitude I receive?" he asked. My cheeks were hot, and I knew they were red with degradation. When I glanced at Becca, she was giggling under her breath at me, still trying to stay placid as she read to the children. My humiliation was her amusement, and yet I fathomed that her heart was kinder than what she had displayed to me during our meeting earlier.

During this exchange of glance and giggle, General Frommer recognized our interchange. "Ahh... you're smitten with the young lady, are you?" He winked and continued without my answer. "I'll grant you this one blunder this time, but the next, it's back to your pup tent."

I swallowed my pride, for I did not care to be anywhere but in the presence of this woman. I resolved to remain in the house.

Activity in full swing, Union soldiers mingled among Southern civilians. Many Vicksburg residents were jailed during our takeover, as they refused to stay out of our way. They would rather be confined to a jail cell than pledge allegiance to any Yankee. The general population of the town, however, were women, children, and elderly folk. The only white men around were aged, or Confederate soldiers who had returned home as invalids.

❧❧❧❧

Shortly after my first meeting with Becca, I received a fresh, new uniform. I had been mortified at introducing myself to her in my physical condition. Filthy. My uniform was in tatters and my body smelled repugnant. Fortunately, I was in one of the wealthiest plantation homes in Mississippi, and they possessed the most beautiful powder room which included a tub. With the newfound knowledge of a lock on the door, I proceeded in filling the tub with water. Digging through my haversack, I found a small bottle of fragrant oil and poured the rest of its contents in as well.

I disrobed, taking great care in removing the bandage wrap I used to strap down my breasts. It, too, was filthy, but I had been saving an unused one for just this opportunity. I dipped one foot into the tepid water, getting acclimated to it before finally submerging my entire body. It felt divine to soak in clean, perfumed water. Inhaling deeply, I relaxed, closed my eyes, and exhaled completely, discovering a peace I had not felt for months now. The morbid images of war that had occupied space in my mind dissipated for the moment. My father's death, the death of Violet's and my love, all vanquished as I was cleaned of all earthly pain and suffering, even if only temporarily.

Without being aware, I fell asleep. It was the soundest sleep I had since...I couldn't remember. There were no bombs exploding directly near my ear, and the constant fear of whizzing Minié balls had all but disappeared. I didn't know how long I slumbered, but much to my dismay, when I awoke, a fresh towel sat folded neatly on a chair by the tub.

I snapped forward, rose to a sitting position, and splashed water sporadically. My heart beat wildly, and I scanned the room in search of someone, anyone. No one was there, but it was apparent that someone had a key to the locked door. Someone had let themselves in and, obviously, discovered that I was a woman. My breasts unmistakably protruded from the bath water. I was now vulnerable to an unidentified person in this house.

Fear overwhelmed me. The idea that someone knew my secret unnerved me to no end. I stood up in the tub and stepped out, beads of water dripping from my clean skin. Grabbing the towel that was placed there for me, I dried my face, my body, and my hair. I searched everywhere for the dirty bandage I had used for months, but could not find it. My anxiety level hadn't been this high for quite some time, and my mind ran in circles seeking a solution. It wasn't that I didn't have another bandage; I had a clean one in my haversack. It was that I wondered where the dirty one was. Did my towel fairy poach my bandage as well? Twas a mystery I could not comprehend.

I bound my breasts and donned my fresh uniform. Looking in the mirror, I placed my kepi on my head. My face was still young, and I, unable to grow whiskers, started to feel irrational over my situation. I buttoned my jacket, straightened my collar, and attempted to convince myself that all was well. I left the powder room not knowing if I would be apprehended by my superiors and removed from service for being a woman posing as a man.

❧❧❧❧

Every look I received as I walked down the hall was sure to seal my fate. Paranoia impeded me from keeping eye contact, and my head and eyes averted downward with each passing, assumed stare. Soldiers were in and out of the house with various orders, but when I entered the parlor for a second time that day, Becca was no longer present. Instead, I had the uncomfortable pleasure of meeting the rest of her family. The plantation mistress introduced herself. "My name is Theodora Livingston, and I am only introducing you to my family so that you may stay out of their way." She sauntered over to me, looked me in my eyes, and said, "I am the plantation mistress. You will address me as Mistress Thea. My husband, Daniel Livingston, is an officer in the Confederate Army. In his stead, any and all inquiries shall be directed to me." She glared at me, looking me up and down. "Do

I make myself clear?"

General Frommer interrupted. "You do realize the United States government has just seized your house and property, yes?" He was clearly puzzled by her arrogance, as if somehow her favored side had won the struggle for Vicksburg.

She snapped her head and fixed her icy stare from me to him. "This city may belong to you now, but this house is mine. Let us go about our business, and we will make sure you are fed more appropriately than the Army ever could."

Reminiscing over our recent famine, with intermittent rations getting through to our lines, he consented to her. "All right then. We are in congruence. Go on with your introductions."

She gestured toward one of two girls seated on the sofa. "This is Loretta. She's my youngest. Thirteen years of age, with a sharp tongue full of derision." The child scoffed and rolled her eyes. Next, she waved her hand toward the other girl. "This is my oldest child, Harriet, or Hattie for short. She's twenty-four with a husband, Chauncy Stuart, who's also in the Confederate Army. They have three children of their own." She pointed to each and named them off as if in roll call. "James, Nathaniel, and Abigail."

Droplets of perspiration formed on my forehead, and my palms became clammy, anticipating at any moment that one of them would step forward and accuse me of being an imposter.

"This is Thaddeus." She introduced the young man next to her as she petted the top of his head. "Thaddeus is nineteen years of age, and a Southern war hero. He took a Minié ball to his shin at Shiloh. He was carrying his brother, Richard, over his shoulder in an attempt to save him. Richard had been shot in the chest by a Yankee rifle, and when Thaddeus lifted him and ran, he took a shot to his leg. It shattered his entire limb and it could not be recovered. I lost my Richard. He bled out from his wound. But how fortunate I was to welcome home my remaining son."

Thaddeus appeared bitter at what took place at Shiloh. He wasn't able to save his brother's life, and he came home half the man he was when he left. I could feel his cold stare on me, his eyes squinting into a scowl. Swearing he was the knower of my secret, I turned to exit the room. But as I turned, I spun right into Becca, who was just entering the parlor.

"Oh! I...I am sorry, miss." I stumbled over my words from the swarm of nerves that invaded my stomach any time she was near. Our eyes held each other's gaze for a brief moment before we were hurled back into the present.

"And this, of course, is my niece, Becca. She is my brother's daughter. Having never married, she moved in with us four years ago to help with the children. Imagine, twenty-three, absolutely lovely, and without one prospect of marriage? That was until just recently. A rough but dashing Confederate guerilla asked for her hand. He stayed on with us as an overseer when the rest of the Army retreated. We're waiting for her father to arrive from Georgia so that they may wed."

My heart was crushed at this news, and I left the parlor stricken with melancholy. I strode toward the front door in need of air, but as I reached for the doorknob, a voice came from behind me. "You'll need to cease looking at me as you do." I turned to find Becca standing there.

"Pardon?" I asked, a bit befuddled.

"I see the way you look at me, with desire in your eyes. It must stop. My fiancé will not tolerate it, I'm sure. And quite frankly, I don't want a Yankee to think of me in that manner."

She had put me in my place, and as unwarranted as it was, I obliged. "Indeed. I've no intention of disrespecting you, my lady, nor your fiancé."

"I am not your lady, and you will address me as Miss Becca."

"All right then." I tipped my hat one last time and bid her adieu. "Miss Becca." Through the front door I went. I left the house that claimed my secret and strolled through the tent city that had risen in just a short time.

❧❧❧❧

The mail was being handed out, and a wide smile grew across my face when I saw one addressed to me. It was from Sadie. Ahh…my rare piece of normal. How a prostitute from Memphis had become my normal, I had no idea. I tore open the letter, unfolded it, and read the two pages carefully, and with much joy. She spoke of a piece of land not far from Memphis. One thousand acres and plenty of ground to build a house. It was ideal farmland, and she once again inquired about the debt I owed her for keeping my identity secret. The jubilance she felt over the anticipation of changing her unfavorable existence came to life in the entire content of her correspondence.

I obtained a writing implement, a piece of stationery, and wandered back up to the veranda, stepping up to and settling on the porch swing. Gently rocking back and forth, I composed the renewal of my promise to her, insisting she had my word of honor.

She meant something to me and I wished to take care of her. She—Sadie, the prostitute from Memphis—was my family. And so, I pledged these things to her in my epistle.

While I was fixated in writing, I was rattled back to the present. A burly man, sloppy and unkempt in appearance, tramped and rumbled up the front steps, forcefully pushing the door open and entering the premises. Not being familiar with this man as a family member, I sprang from my seat and hastened into the house behind him.

"Halt," I shouted, but to no avail. He kept right on moving through the house. "Stop! Who are you?"

The devil himself may have well turned around, for when he did, his eye held the hatred and darkness of such said beast. It was Clifford T. Booker, the Rebel guerilla who killed Yankees for his own demented amusement. He had practically raped Sadie in front of my very eyes. A sinister fellow with a malign agenda. His heart was black, and I had no clue as to why he was here.

"I'm the overseer here, and I've come in from the fields to see my fiancée, and maybe fetch me some tea," he answered, his eyes burning a hole into the goodness of my soul. He stepped toward me and tilted his head downward to finish intimidating me. His sheer size was daunting enough, but his gruff voice was that of a snarl and growl. "My name is Clifford T. Booker, and you'll do best to keep out of my way."

With a deep, chilling stare, he turned and started for the parlor. His heavy boots trod into the room, and I heard his voice and that of a female. I crept forward and peeked around the wall, horrified to see him grab and embrace Becca. "No," I whispered out loud, aghast at the sight of his grubby, filthy hands rubbing on her. As he drew her into his arms for a stolen kiss, I abruptly entered the room. Becca gasped and pushed him away.

Realizing who I was, she scolded me. "How dare you walk into a room without first announcing yourself?"

"I was…I…" I stuttered and stumbled over my words. Although she was remiss with me, her eyes told a different story. Her eyes, like two endless, swirling skies, cascaded shades of dark and light blues over one another in an effort to allow the sun out, or else cast an awful storm in its place. She wanted me to see the iciness, the coldness, but I saw deeper than the superficial attitude she portrayed. No, her eyes were as warm and inviting as a warm bath. Like the tide, she was pulled in different directions, seemingly tormented. Perhaps she hid her sadness in the pit of her breast. I saw the sadness that no one else bothered to see. It was buried gravely beneath the surface.

"Speak up then," she said, attempting to pry out my words.

"I was just checking on you, Miss Becca."

"That won't be necessary. I am not a child."

"But of course. My apologies." Again, I tipped my hat, and returned to the veranda.

⁂

That night, having the privilege of residing in the house, I set up a cot in the parlor. Mistress Thea had already retired for the night, along with the rest of the household. I removed my uniform jacket, leaving my shirt on in the process. I climbed into bed with all but my boots. Lying there, sleep became difficult.

Tossing and turning from one side to the other, I could not get comfortable. I finally settled on my back and closed my eyes.

The house made creaking sounds I was not accustomed to, and the insects and reptiles outside sang their nocturnal love songs. As I was about to fall into slumber, I faintly heard a door close on the second level, where all of the bedchambers were. Ignoring it, I re-closed my eyes. But again, I heard noise coming from upstairs. Light footsteps, and then the sound of someone trying to quietly come down the staircase, prompted me to sit upright on my cot. It was dark except for the moonlight shining in through the windows. I caught the silhouette of a woman scampering toward the back door.

Not yet sure of who it was, curiosity got the better of me, and I rose from my bed and slipped into my boots. Tacitly, I scrambled to the same door, peeking out to see the woman headed for a hill that sat in near proximity to the house. I followed. Through a clump of trees positioned between, I trailed her. When she arrived at her destination, I hid behind one of the tall oaks, and observed as she pried a piece of wood from a giant hole in the side of the hill and entered. This, obviously, was the cave they sought refuge in during the siege of the town.

I made a dash for a bush that sat at the entrance of the cave and peered in, seeing a candle lit by none other than Becca Chamberlain. The cave was furnished with furniture from the big house, as this had undoubtedly been their residence for six weeks. She moved a small bookcase over about a half a foot, and dug the earth below with a small spade she had handy inside. After scooping out a rather deep hole, she reached in and pulled from it a brown leather journal. She sat at a small desk and unwound the leather sash attached to it. Dabbing the pen in the inkwell, she began writing.

I spied on her for a time, admiring her beauty as I did and longing to tell her such. As she wrote, she periodically paused, clearly in thought, before taking pen to paper once more. The candlelight cast enough glow to expose the details of her lovely face. Concern was heavy on her, as her eyebrows drew together and her lips trembled at what she wrote on that page. She was in distress and I did not know why.

Just as I was about to return to the house, feeling as though I was intruding on her, she dropped the pen, placed her face in her hands, and started to sob. She attempted to remain calm, forcing her emotions down, but she was unable to control the whimpering that escaped her throat. Her whole body shook with sadness, and all I wanted to do was hold her close to me and tell her all would be okay. Restraint was something I prided myself on, a necessity under my own circumstances, so I pried myself from the bush I hid behind and took a step in the direction from whence I came. Misfortune was the stick that broke under the weight of my boot, and when I looked up, she saw me. Having made eye contact, I was sure she was about to chastise me for lingering and sneaking around her.

However, she merely gave me a pretentious smile, trying to veil and cover her wet face, full of tears. I simply looked at her, then at the ground, my attempt at allowing her that cover in a bid to respect her. I felt as if I had invaded her privacy in a moment I was not meant to see. Off into the darkness I strode, between the trees, and back into the big house. I lay in my cot, completely awake until I heard her return as well, climb the steps, and retire to her bedroom for the rest of the night. I hungered to know what burdened her heart so heavily. I wished to take that pain from her and carry it in my bosom to relieve her heartache, relieve her of any burden and toll.

This war had taken a toll on me, not only the physical war going on in our country but the war in my head. Up to this point I had been able to keep my secret, even if it had been difficult. However, someone in this house had knowledge of my truth, and keeping calm about it had been impossible. By all appearances I was confident and in control, but on the inside I was uncomfortable in my own skin. My paranoia about the situation was becoming unsustainable, and knowing that Clifford was here and betrothed to Becca made my heart even heavier. The immoral man was a situation all in himself.

But among the many things I had learned about myself through the hardship and toil of battle, I had also realized my need for love. I ached and longed for it. This solitary life I had chosen for myself was wearing thin, and Becca reminded me of all that I was missing. That connection. That connection that binds one person to another, that intimacy. Violet was once the image of what I thought love looked like, but that image had shifted and now looked like Becca. Witnessing her own secret sorrow had given me cause to think we had more in common than what was visible on the surface. At least, I hoped it was so. I wouldn't be satisfied until I knew her, all of her. Perhaps once this war was over there would be hope for a better day, a better life for me. I fell asleep dreaming of what it would feel like to hold her in my arms.

If you liked this book?

Reviews help a new author get discovered and if you have enjoyed this book, please do the author the honor of posting a review on Goodreads, Amazon, Barnes & Noble or anywhere you purchased the book. Or perhaps share a posting on your social media sites or spread the word to your friends.

About the author

TL Dickerson resides in southern New Jersey with her beautiful wife, Gail, and their lazy housecat, Sweetie. When she's not writing, she enjoys spending time on the beach where she finds a peace one can only find at the ocean. One of her favorite pastimes is studying the American Civil War and visiting as many Civil War battlefield sites as possible. Her most prized possessions are artifacts she's collected from the era. She loves horror and comedy flicks, and her all-time favorite sitcom is Friends. She enjoys a wide variety of music, but her favored preference is old-school rap and hip-hop. There are a lot of female rappers she likes, but her favorite is Missy Elliott. Above all else, TL makes a mean pot of gravy. Not sauce, gravy.

TL has written two previous books to Hearts Under Siege. Writing in the Lesbian Fiction, Romance/Erotica genre, she has two self-published novels, the debut Servicing the Rich, and sophomore effort A Breath in Time. Both are available at Amazon and on Kindle. Keep watch for her upcoming Coffield Chronicles book, Hearts Under Fire, a sequel to Hearts Under Siege.

Other books by Sapphire Authors

Last First Kiss: A Passport to Love Romance – ISBN – 978-1-948232-95-1

Alessia Cavalii is a rising star in the competitive international wine scene, and one of only twenty-six female master sommeliers in the world. Her home is a renovated winery on the windswept coast of Italy, she has a career she loves, and she is finally free of a toxic relationship. But Alessia is hiding a dangerous secret—one that could, in a second, shatter the life she's built. Parker Haven is a captain in the U.S. Army and stationed at the NATO military camp near Salerno. An investigator with the Military Police, she's pulled in to help solve a string of murders in the city and finds herself inexplicably drawn into Alessia's world. As the intrigue surrounding the case—and the alluring Alessia—spins more and more out of control, Parker realizes she may have to choose between her military career and the woman she's falling for. Do we ever truly know the people we love?

A storm's brewing on the horizon. Can Addie and Greyson weather it, or will it blow them over?

Killer Spring – ISBN – 978-1-948232-39-5

In this sequel to Killer Winter, Leah Samuels has moved to the planet Xing to get away from the killer winters on her home world. Her investigative firm is hired to find the killer of the daughter of one of the richest families on the planet when the police are unable to find the murderer. With meticulous attention to detail, Leah and her team delve into the crime, pursuing leads that weren't even on the radar of the police. They encounter intrigue, danger, and deception while trying to unravel the mystery, all afforded them by a corrupt system and a powerful underworld.

When she meets the sister of the murdered woman, Jardain Bensington, Leah falls into lust, something she didn't think was possible until it happens to her. Her mind tells her to walk away, but the rest of her body, including her heart, tells her to take a chance on Jardain. But Jardain's playgirl reputation and her possible involvement in her sister's murder threaten to keep them apart, despite the mutual attraction.

Join the Black Orchid Investigations team in this second in a four-book series featuring Leah Samuels.

Blueprint for Romance: A Garriety Romance – ISBN – 978-1-948232-71-5

After the death of her husband, Dylan Lake's ability to trust in others is shattered. Her life is thrust into turmoil between caring for Emma, her seven-year old handicapped child, and working hard to make ends meet. Dylan doesn't have time to pursue a romantic relationship. Finding that one special person only happens in dreams. When fate keeps throwing Dylan and Kat together, Dylan finds her attraction to Kat something she can't ignore. Will her trust issues stop her from letting Kat into her and Emma's life? Leaving her old job and moving halfway across the country were the scariest things Kat Anderson had ever done. Starting a new life and career takes priority over any foolish notion of a fairy-tale future of romance and love. Kat's attraction to Dylan is time taken away from building a new business. Can Kat juggle love and duty to find her Happy Ever After? Welcome back to Garriety, the town with an open heart, and home to some of the quirky and warm characters from Add Romance and Mix. Join Kat and Dylan on their quest for true romance with a little help from Kat's sister Briley and her family, along with a host of new characters.

Faithful Valor – ISBN – 978-1-948232-85-2

Sometimes danger isn't found on a battleground—it's sitting at your front door. Nic Caldwell is back Stateside, working the job she was supposed to have before her most recent deployment, and living her best life at home. At least she thought she would be, except her PTSD is always in the background, dragging her back to her tour in Afghanistan. As she struggles to control her demons privately, her public life with Claire is almost picture perfect. However, a picture can't show everything hiding just under the surface. Claire Monroe has the love of her life back in one piece—almost. She's trying to help Nic adjust to her new normal both physically and emotionally while also going back to school and raising their daughter, Grace. With all the difficulties Nic's re-entry poses along with the new challenges of being an adult student, she wonders how she can guide them back to their old life while building a new one for herself. Cece Ramirez has decided that the Army has served its purpose and she is ready for a new chapter in her professional and personal life. Retiring from active duty and moving on to a new role as a police officer on a college campus, she realizes that she's traded camo, discipline, and rifles for book bags, bikes, and rowdy post-adolescents. While she and the students at Cal State Monterey Bay might be the same age, their pasts are vastly different, and the transition from soldier to college cop may not be as smooth as she hopes. When a chance encounter at a near-base shopette challenges Nic's authority and leaves her and her family in potential peril, Cece and Claire must pull together to back Nic up in peacetime, and right at home.

To Be Loved – ISBN – 978-1-948232-79-1

A dead body, women and kids in peril, treachery at every turn—no problem for the close-knit sexagenarian friends of the Silver Series, Dory, Robby, Jill and Charlene! When a calm evening walk leads Dory to suspect bad news is happening right next door in her placid neighborhood, and when a waif comes under Jill's wing, routine life takes a vacation. And when a corpse points toward a suspect who's far from virginal in character, and seems to link to the waif and the bad news, well! All bets are off. The women rally to defeat evil and correct injustice, helped with a generous serving of karma from a very unexpected source. Along the way, they work with and for the police, sometimes in—ah, unorthodox—ways. But what are a few more gray hairs to law enforcement when the cause of justice is advanced? They encounter smugglers in the devil's oldest crime, street-smart kids wiser than their years, maids in distress, and unlikely allies in Skid Row. But the persistent four also marshal the vengeance of the angels, through their own

Highland Dew – ISBN – 978-1-948232-11-1

Bryce Andrews, west coast sales director for Global Distillers and Distribution, is tired of the corporate hamster wheel. She needs a change.

A craft whisky trade show offers her inspiration and a chance to revisit Scotland and the majestic scenery of the Speyside region—best known for the "Whisky Trail." Bryce and her coworker, Reggie Ballard, need to find a wholly original whisky for their international distribution division by visiting a number of small distillers.

A blind curve, a dangling sign, and weed-choked driveway draw Bryce directly into a truly unique opportunity. She discovers a struggling family, a shuttered distillery, and a spitfire of a daughter called home to care for her confused father.

Fiona McDougall—the only child and heir to the MacDougall & Son legacy, had her career teaching in Edinburgh curtailed by fate…or serendipity.

When the stars finally align, the two women work together to resurrect a dream for themselves and the family business—if they can weather the storms of unscrupulous business practices in the competitive whisky market.